THE SHADOW OUT OF TIME

THE SHADOW OUT OF TIME

H. P. LOVECRAFT

ILLUSTRATIONS BY

PETE VON SHOLLY

INTRODUCTION BY

S. T. JOSHI

THE PULPS LIBRARY

EX
LIBRIS

HOWARD
PHILLIPS
LOVECRAFT

The Shadow out of Time

The corrected texts used in this and other titles in the PS library of H. P. Lovecraft's work © 1984–1986 by S. T. Joshi.

Cover and Interior Illustrations
Copyright © Pete Von Sholly 2015

Introduction © S. T. Joshi 2015

The Vanity of Existence in "The Shadow out of Time" © Paul Montelone 1996

The Shadow out of Plastic © Pete Von Sholly 2015

"The Shadow out of Time" as Lovecraftian Horror © W. H. Pugmire 2014

Published in February 2015 by The Pulps Library, an imprint of PS Publishing Ltd., by arrangement with S. T. Joshi.

FIRST PS EDITION

ISBN
978-1-848637-34-4

Design & Layout by Eric Nolen-Weathington

Printed and bound in England by the T. J. International

PS Publishing Ltd
Grosvenor House
1 New Road
Hornsea, HU18 1PG
England

editor@pspublishing.co.uk
www.pspublishing.co.uk

Contents

Introduction

by S. T. Joshi

"The Shadow out of Time" was Lovecraft's last major tale, written between November 10, 1934, and February 22, 1935. This relatively long period of composition betrays the difficulties that Lovecraft faced at a time when his confidence in his own abilities as a fiction writer was at a low ebb. Ever since *At the Mountains of Madness* had been rejected by *Weird Tales* in 1931, Lovecraft had been plagued with doubts about his capacity to write fiction effectively. A number of tales during this period required several drafts before they were completed, and "The Shadow out of Time" was no different.

In mid-November 1934, Lovecraft wrote to a friend: "I developed that story *mistily and allusively* in 16 pages, but it was no go. Thin and unconvincing, with the climactic revelation wholly unjustified by the hash of visions preceding it." It is difficult to imagine what such a truncated version might have been like. Lovecraft probably realised that the history of the Great Race—those extraterrestrial entities whose minds hop from one species to the next—was really the heart of the narrative, and so he expanded his draft into a full-fledged novella. He produced a second version in December, but admitted that it failed to satisfy him; so he started over, finally finishing the third version early in 1935.

A number of literary influences operated on the novella, but in such a way as to demonstrate the profound originality of Lovecraft's conception and execution of the tale. The basic idea of mind-exchange may have been derived from H. B. Drake's novel *The Shadowy Thing* (1928; published in the UK in 1925 as *The Remedy*); this novel had already been a partial inspiration on Lovecraft's earlier story "The Thing on the Doorstep" (1933). However, the notion of *mind-exchange over time* appears to have been Lovecraft's own. As early as 1930, he had discussed a plot idea about time travel in various letters to Clark Ashton Smith, writing: "One baffling thing that could be introduced is to have a modern man discover, among documents exhumed from some prehistoric buried city, a mouldering papyrus or parchment *written in English, & in his own handwriting.*" This is, of course, an encapsulation of the spectacular climax of the story. In 1932 he had outlined the idea of an extraterrestrial species "who gained a knowledge of all arts & sciences by sending thought-streams ahead to drain the minds of men in future ages—angling in time, as it were."

It is important to note this passage because, the next year, Lovecraft saw the film *Berkeley Square* (1933), in which a man from the twentieth century appears to be possessed by the mind of his ancestor from the eighteenth century. Lovecraft was struck by the film, seeing it four times; perhaps he recognised it as a strange parallel to his own unpublished novel *The Case of Charles Dexter Ward* (1927). But the film's idea of psychic possession over time had already been anticipated in the letter of 1932.

The remarkable thing about "The Shadow out of Time" is its relative absence of actual terror. This was clearly by design, as Lovecraft was shifting away from supernatural horror to awe and wonder in many of his later narratives. To be sure, the discovery by the narrator, Nathaniel Wingate Peaslee, that his body had been possessed by the mind of a member of the Great Race engenders a spasm of existential horror in him for a time; but he gradually becomes reconciled to the fact, and the idea that his own mind (in the body of his psychic captor) could explore the immense library of the Great Race's city in Australia is an extraordinarily enticing one for anyone with a thirst for knowledge and history. Lovecraft does turn up the emotional volume toward the end, writing in an increasingly frenzied manner as Peaslee, facing increasing evidence that the Great Race's city actually exists under the sands of the Australian desert, races to come upon the final proof that his "dreams" of being psychically possessed were based on actual events—the document that he himself, in the body of his captor, had written millions of years ago. Peaslee does find this document but conveniently loses it upon his return to the surface; but he now knows that all his "dreams" were reflections of a mind-shattering reality.

"The Shadow out of Time" was submitted to *Astounding Stories* by Donald Wandrei, only days after Julius Schwartz had successfully marketed *At the Mountains of Madness* to the magazine. Editor F. Orlin Tremaine accepted the novella readily, paying Lovecraft $280 for it. In his letters Lovecraft—who had been outraged at the manner in which *At the Mountains of Madness* had been tampered with by the *Astounding* editorial staff—stated that "The Shadow out of Time" did not suffer a similar fate; but the recent discovery of his handwritten manuscript belies that claim. Lovecraft himself did not prepare the typescript; he was so discouraged as to the quality of the tale that he could not bring himself to do so. His young friend R. H. Barlow, hosting Lovecraft at his Florida home in the summer of 1935, surreptitiously typed the story for him, but he made many stenographic errors. *Astounding* then proceeded to chop up Lovecraft's long, leisurely paragraphs in exactly the same way as it had done with *At the Mountains of Madness*, and also made other changes, although there were no actual cuts in the text as there were in the Antarctic novel. But the handwritten manuscript—which for more than a half-century was thought to be lost or destroyed, but unexpected surfaced in 1994—has made possible the restoration of the text, so that we can now read it as Lovecraft intended.

Like *At the Mountains of Madness*, this novella is one of the more visual in Lovecraft's fictional output, and Pete Von Sholly has brought his customary skill in portraying key elements of the text. Whether it be Peaslee's strange dreams during his five-year "amnesia," or the cosmic history of the Great Race on this planet and elsewhere, or the Great Race's hideous battles with nameless entities (the Blind Beings) even more bizarre than themselves, or Peaslee's final mad, solitary scramble through the barren Australian desert, Von Sholly has captured the visual essence of a novella that spans both infinities of time and incalculable gulfs of space in a sprawling narrative that has inspired readers of horror and science fiction alike.

THE SHADOW OUT OF TIME

I

After twenty-two years of nightmare and terror, saved only by a desperate conviction of the mythical source of certain impressions, I am unwilling to vouch for the truth of that which I think I found in Western Australia on the night of July 17–18, 1935. There is reason to hope that my experience was wholly or partly an hallucination—for which, indeed, abundant causes existed. And yet, its realism was so hideous that I sometimes find hope impossible. If the thing did happen, then man must be prepared to accept notions of the cosmos, and of his own place in the seething vortex of time, whose merest mention is paralysing. He must, too, be placed on guard against a specific lurking peril which, though it will never engulf the whole race, may impose monstrous and unguessable horrors upon certain venturesome members of it. It is for this latter reason that I urge, with all the force of my being, a final abandonment of all attempts at unearthing those fragments of unknown, primordial masonry which my expedition set out to investigate.

Assuming that I was sane and awake, my experience on that night was such as has befallen no man before. It was, moreover, a frightful confirmation of all I had sought to dismiss as myth and dream. Mercifully there is no proof, for in my fright I lost the awesome object which would—if real and brought out of that noxious abyss—have formed irrefutable evidence. When I came upon the horror I was alone—and I have up to now told no one about it. I could not stop the others from digging in its direction, but chance and the shifting sand have so far saved them from finding it. Now I must formulate some definitive statement—not only for the sake of my own mental balance, but to warn such others as may read it seriously.

These pages—much in whose earlier parts will be familiar to close readers of the general and scientific press—are written in the cabin of the ship that is bringing me home. I shall give them to my son, Prof. Wingate Peaslee of Miskatonic University—the only member of my family who stuck to me after my queer amnesia of long ago, and the man best informed on the inner facts of my case. Of all living persons, he is least likely to ridicule what I shall tell of that fateful night. I did not enlighten him orally before sailing, because I think he had better have the revelation in written form. Reading and re-reading at leisure will leave with him a more convincing picture than my confused tongue could hope to convey. He can do as he thinks best with this account—shewing it, with suitable comment, to any quarters where it will be likely to accomplish good. It is for the sake of such readers as are unfamiliar with the earlier phases of my case that I am prefacing the revelation itself with a fairly ample summary of its background.

My name is Nathaniel Wingate Peaslee, and those who recall the newspaper tales of a generation back—or the letters and articles in psychological journals six or seven years ago—will know who and what I am. The press was filled with the details of my strange amnesia in 1908–13, and much was made of the traditions of horror, madness, and witchcraft which lurk behind the ancient Massachusetts town then and now forming my place of residence. Yet I would have it known that there is nothing whatever of the mad or sinister in my heredity and early life. This is a highly important fact in view of the shadow which fell so suddenly upon me from outside sources. It may be that centuries of dark brooding had given to crumbling, whisper-haunted Arkham a peculiar vulnerability as regards such shadows—though even this seems doubtful in the light of those other cases which I later came to study. But the chief point is that my own ancestry and background are altogether normal. What came, came from *somewhere else*—where, I even now hesitate to assert in plain words.

I am the son of Jonathan and Hannah (Wingate) Peaslee, both of wholesome old Haverhill stock. I was born and reared in Haverhill—at the old homestead in Boardman Street near Golden Hill—and did not go to Arkham till I entered Miskatonic University at the age of eighteen. That was in 1889. After my graduation I studied economics at Harvard, and came back to Miskatonic as Instructor of Political Economy in 1895. For thirteen years more my life ran smoothly and happily. I married Alice Keezar of Haverhill in 1896, and my three children, Robert K., Wingate, and Hannah, were born in 1898, 1900, and 1903, respectively. In 1898 I became an associate professor, and in 1902 a full professor. At no time had I the least interest in either occultism or abnormal psychology.

It was on Thursday, May 14, 1908, that the queer amnesia came. The thing was quite sudden, though later I realised that certain brief, glimmering visions of several hours previous—chaotic visions which disturbed me greatly because they were so unprecedented—must have formed premonitory symptoms. My head was aching, and I had a singular feeling—altogether new to me—that someone else was trying to get possession of my thoughts.

The collapse occurred about 10:20 a.m., while I was conducting a class in Political Economy VI—history and present tendencies of economics—for juniors and a few sophomores. I began to see strange shapes before my eyes, and to feel that I was in a grotesque room other than the classroom. My thoughts and speech wandered from my subject, and the students saw that something was gravely amiss. Then I slumped down, unconscious in my chair, in a stupor from which no one could arouse me. Nor did my rightful faculties again look out upon the daylight of our normal world for five years, four months, and thirteen days.

It is, of course, from others that I have learned what followed. I shewed no sign of consciousness for sixteen and a half hours, though removed to my home at 27 Crane St. and given the best of medical attention. At 3 a.m. May 15 my eyes opened and I began to speak, but before long the doctors and my family were thoroughly frightened by the trend of my expression and language. It was clear that I had no remembrance of my identity or of my past, though for some reason I seemed anxious to conceal this lack of knowledge. My eyes gazed strangely at the persons around me, and the flexions of my facial muscles were altogether unfamiliar.

Even my speech seemed awkward and foreign. I used my vocal organs clumsily and gropingly, and my diction had a curiously stilted quality, as if I had laboriously learned the English language from books. The pronunciation was barbarously alien, whilst the idiom seemed to include both scraps of curious archaism and expressions of a wholly incomprehensible cast. Of the latter one in particular was very potently—even terrifiedly—recalled by the youngest of the physicians twenty years afterward. For at that late period such a phrase began to have an actual currency—first in England and then in the United States—and though of much complexity and indisputable newness, it reproduced in every least particular the mystifying words of the strange Arkham patient of 1908.

Physical strength returned at once, although I required an odd amount of re-education in the use of my hands, legs, and bodily apparatus in general. Because of this and other handicaps inherent in the mnemonic lapse, I was for some time kept under strict medical care. When I saw that my attempts to conceal the lapse had failed, I admitted it openly, and became eager for information of all sorts. Indeed, it seemed to the doctors that I had lost interest in my proper personality as soon as I found the case of amnesia accepted as a natural thing. They noticed that my chief efforts were to master certain points in history, science, art, language, and folklore—some of them tremendously abstruse, and some childishly simple—which remained, very oddly in many cases, outside my consciousness.

At the same time they noticed that I had an inexplicable command of many almost unknown sorts of knowledge—a command which I seemed to wish to hide rather than display. I would inadvertently refer, with casual assurance, to specific events in dim ages outside the range of accepted history—passing off such references as a jest when I saw the surprise they created. And I had a way of speaking of the future which two or three times caused actual fright. These uncanny flashes soon ceased to appear, though some observers laid their vanishment more to a certain furtive caution on my part than to any waning of the strange knowledge behind them. Indeed, I seemed anomalously avid to absorb the speech, customs, and perspectives of the age around me; as if I were a studious traveller from a far, foreign land.

As soon as permitted, I haunted the college library at all hours; and shortly began to arrange for those odd travels, and special courses at American and European universities, which evoked so much comment during the next few years. I did not at any time suffer from a lack of learned contacts, for my case had a mild celebrity among the psychologists of the period. I was lectured upon as a typical example of secondary personality—even though I seemed to puzzle the lecturers now and then with some bizarre symptom or some queer trace of carefully veiled mockery.

Of real friendliness, however, I encountered little. Something in my aspect and speech seemed to excite vague fears and aversions in everyone I met, as if I were a being infinitely removed from all that is normal and healthful. This idea of a black, hidden horror connected with incalculable gulfs of some sort of *distance* was oddly widespread and persistent. My own family formed no exception. From the moment of my strange waking my wife had regarded me with extreme horror and loathing, vowing that I was some utter alien usurping the body of her husband. In 1910 she obtained a legal divorce, nor would she ever consent to see me even after my return to normalcy in 1913. These feelings were shared by my elder son and my small daughter, neither of whom I have ever seen since.

Only my second son Wingate seemed able to conquer the terror and repulsion which my change aroused. He indeed felt that I was a stranger, but though only eight years old held fast to a faith that my proper self would return. When it did return he sought me out, and the courts gave me his custody. In succeeding years he helped me with the studies to which I was driven, and today at thirty-five he is a professor of psychology at Miskatonic. But I do not wonder at the horror I caused—for certainly, the mind, voice, and facial expression of the being that awaked on May 15, 1908 were not those of Nathaniel Wingate Peaslee.

I will not attempt to tell much of my life from 1908 to 1913, since readers may glean all the outward essentials—as I largely had to do—from files of old newspapers and scientific journals. I was given charge of my funds, and spent them slowly and on the whole wisely, in travel and in study at various centres of learning. My travels, however, were singular in the extreme; involving long visits to remote and desolate places. In 1909 I spent a month in the Himalayas, and in 1911 aroused much attention through a camel trip into the unknown deserts of Arabia. What happened on those journeys I have never been able to learn. During the summer of 1912 I chartered a ship and sailed in the Arctic north of Spitzbergen, afterward shewing signs of disappointment. Later in that year I spent weeks alone beyond the limits of previous or subsequent exploration in the vast limestone cavern systems of western Virginia—black labyrinths so complex that no retracing of my steps could even be considered.

My sojourns at the universities were marked by abnormally rapid assimilation, as if the secondary personality had an intelligence enormously superior to my own. I have found, also, that my rate of reading and solitary study was phenomenal. I could master every detail of a book merely by glancing over it as fast as I could turn the leaves; while my skill at interpreting complex figures in an instant was veritably awesome. At times there appeared almost ugly reports of my power to influence the thoughts and acts of others, though I seemed to have taken care to minimise displays of this faculty.

Other ugly reports concerned my intimacy with leaders of occultist groups, and scholars suspected of connexion with nameless bands of abhorrent elder-world hierophants. These rumours, though never proved at the time, were doubtless stimulated by the known tenor of some of my reading—for the consultation of rare books at libraries cannot be effected secretly. There is tangible proof—in the form of marginal notes—that I went minutely through such things as the Comte d'Erlette's *Cultes des Goules*, Ludvig Prinn's *De Vermis Mysteriis*, the *Unaussprechlichen Kulten* of von Junzt, the surviving fragments of the puzzling *Book of Eibon*, and the dreaded *Necronomicon* of the mad Arab Abdul Alhazred. Then, too, it is undeniable that a fresh and evil wave of underground cult activity set in about the time of my odd mutation.

In the summer of 1913 I began to display signs of ennui and flagging interest, and to hint to various associates that a change might soon be expected in me. I spoke of returning memories of my earlier life—though most auditors judged me insincere, since all the recollections I gave were casual, and such as might have been learned from my old private papers. About the middle of August I returned to Arkham and reopened my long-closed house in Crane St. Here I installed a mechanism of the most curious aspect, constructed piecemeal by different makers of scientific apparatus in Europe and America, and guarded carefully from the sight of anyone intelligent enough to analyse it. Those who did see it—a workman, a servant, and the new housekeeper—say that it was a queer mixture of rods, wheels, and mirrors, though only about two feet tall, one foot wide, and one foot thick. The central mirror was circular and convex. All this is borne out by such makers of parts as can be located.

On the evening of Friday, September 26, I dismissed the housekeeper and the maid till noon of the next day. Lights burned in the house till late, and a lean, dark, curiously foreign-looking man called in an automobile. It was about 1 a.m. that the lights were last seen. At 2:15 a.m. a policeman observed the place in darkness, but with the stranger's motor still at the curb. By four o'clock the motor was certainly gone. It was at six that a hesitant, foreign voice on the telephone asked Dr. Wilson to call at my house and bring me out of a peculiar faint. This call—a long-distance one—was later traced to a public booth in the North Station in Boston, but no sign of the lean foreigner was ever unearthed.

When the doctor reached my house he found me unconscious in the sitting-room—in an easy-chair with a table drawn up before it. On the polished table-top were scratches shewing where some heavy object had rested. The queer machine was gone, nor was anything afterward heard of it. Undoubtedly the dark, lean foreigner had taken it away. In the library grate were abundant ashes evidently left from the burning of every remaining scrap of paper on which I had written since the advent of the amnesia. Dr. Wilson found my breathing very peculiar, but after an hypodermic injection it became more regular.

At 11:15 a.m., September 27, I stirred vigorously, and my hitherto mask-like face began to shew signs of expression. Dr. Wilson remarked that the expression was not that of my secondary personality, but seemed much like that of my normal self. About 11:30 I muttered some very curious syllables—syllables which seemed unrelated to any human speech. I appeared, too, to struggle against something. Then, just after noon—the housekeeper and the maid having meanwhile returned—I began to mutter in English.

". . . of the orthodox economists of that period, Jevons typifies the prevailing trend toward scientific correlation. His attempt to link the commercial cycle of prosperity and depression with the physical cycle of the solar spots forms perhaps the apex of . . ."

Nathaniel Wingate Peaslee had come back—a spirit in whose time-scale it was still that Thursday morning in 1908, with the economics class gazing up at the battered desk on the platform.

II

My reabsorption into normal life was a painful and difficult process. The loss of over five years creates more complications than can be imagined, and in my case there were countless matters to be adjusted. What I heard of my actions since 1908 astonished and disturbed me, but I tried to view the matter as philosophically as I could. At last regaining custody of my second son Wingate, I settled down with him in the Crane Street house and endeavoured to resume teaching—my old professorship having been kindly offered me by the college.

I began work with the February, 1914, term, and kept at it just a year. By that time I realised how badly my experience had shaken me. Though perfectly sane—I hoped—and with no flaw in my original personality, I had not the nervous energy of the old days. Vague dreams and queer ideas continually haunted me, and when the outbreak of the world war turned my mind to history I found myself thinking of periods and events in the oddest possible fashion.

My conception of *time*—my ability to distinguish between consecutiveness and simultaneousness—seemed subtly disordered; so that I formed chimerical notions about living in one age and casting one's mind all over eternity for knowledge of past and future ages.

The war gave me strange impressions of *remembering* some of its far-off *consequences*—as if I knew how it was coming out and could look *back* upon it in the light of future information. All such quasi-memories were attended with much pain, and with a feeling that some artificial psychological barrier was set against them. When I diffidently hinted to others about my impressions I met with varied responses. Some persons looked uncomfortably at me, but men in the mathematics department spoke of new developments in those theories of relativity—then discussed only in learned circles—which were later to become so famous. Dr. Albert Einstein, they said, was rapidly reducing *time* to the status of a mere dimension.

But the dreams and disturbed feelings gained on me, so that I had to drop my regular work in 1915. Certain of the impressions were taking an annoying shape—giving me the persistent notion that my amnesia had formed some unholy sort of exchange; that the secondary personality had indeed been an intruding force from unknown regions, and that my own personality had suffered displacement. Thus I was driven to vague and frightful speculations concerning the whereabouts of my true self during the years that another had held my body. The curious knowledge and strange conduct of my body's late tenant troubled me more and more as I learned further details from persons, papers, and magazines. Queernesses that had baffled others seemed to harmonise terribly with some background of black knowledge which festered in the chasms of my subconscious. I began to search feverishly for every scrap of information bearing on the studies and travels of *that other one* during the dark years.

Not all of my troubles were as semi-abstract as this. There were the dreams—and these seemed to grow in vividness and concreteness. Knowing how most would regard them, I seldom mentioned them to anyone but my son or certain trusted psychologists, but eventually I commenced a scientific study of other cases in order to see how typical or non-typical such visions might be among amnesia victims. My results, aided by psychologists, historians, anthropologists, and mental specialists of wide experience, and by a study that included all records of split personalities from the days of daemoniac-possession legends to the medically realistic present, at first bothered me more than they consoled me.

I soon found that my dreams had indeed no counterpart in the overwhelming bulk of true amnesia cases. There remained, however, a tiny residue of accounts which for years baffled and shocked me with their parallelism to my own experience. Some of them were bits of ancient folklore; others were case-histories in the annals of medicine; one or two were anecdotes obscurely buried in standard histories. It thus appeared that, while my special kind of affliction was prodigiously rare, instances of it had occurred at long intervals ever since the beginning of man's annals. Some centuries might contain one, two, or three cases; others none—or at least none whose record survived.

The essence was always the same—a person of keen thoughtfulness seized with a strange secondary life and leading for a greater or lesser period an utterly alien existence typified at first by vocal and bodily awkwardness, and later by a wholesale acquisition of scientific, historic, artistic, and anthropological knowledge; an acquisition carried on with feverish zest and with a wholly abnormal absorptive power. Then a sudden return of the rightful consciousness, intermittently plagued ever after with vague unplaceable dreams suggesting fragments of some hideous memory elaborately blotted out. And the close resemblance of those nightmares to my own—even in some of the smallest particulars—left no doubt in my mind of their significantly typical nature. One or two of the cases had an added ring of faint, blasphemous familiarity, as if I had heard of them before through some cosmic channel too morbid and frightful to contemplate. In three instances there was specific mention of such an unknown machine as had been in my house before the second change.

Another thing that cloudily worried me during my investigation was the somewhat greater frequency of cases where a brief, elusive glimpse of the typical nightmares was afforded to persons not visited with well-defined amnesia. These persons were largely of mediocre mind or less—some so primitive that they could scarcely be thought of as vehicles for abnormal scholarship and preternatural mental acquisitions. For a second they would be fired with alien force—then a backward lapse and a thin, swift-fading memory of un-human horrors.

There had been at least three such cases during the past half century—one only fifteen years before. Had something been *groping blindly through time* from some unsuspected abyss in Nature? Were these faint cases monstrous, sinister *experiments* of a kind and authorship utterly beyond sane belief? Such were a few of the formless speculations of my weaker hours—fancies abetted by myths which my studies uncovered. For I could not doubt but that certain persistent legends of immemorial antiquity, apparently unknown to the victims and physicians connected with recent amnesia cases, formed a striking and awesome elaboration of memory lapses such as mine.

Of the nature of the dreams and impressions which were growing so clamorous I still almost fear to speak. They seemed to savour of madness, and at times I believed I was indeed going mad. Was there a special type of delusion afflicting those who had suffered lapses of memory? Conceivably, the efforts of the subconscious mind to fill up a perplexing blank with pseudo-memories might give rise to strange imaginative vagaries. This, indeed (though an alternative folklore theory finally seemed to me more plausible), was the belief of many of the alienists who helped me in my search for parallel cases, and who shared my puzzlement at the exact resemblances sometimes discovered. They did not call the condition true insanity, but classed it rather among neurotic disorders. My course in trying to track it down and analyse it, instead of vainly seeking to dismiss or forget it, they heartily endorsed as correct according to the best psychological principles. I especially valued the advice of such physicians as had studied me during my possession by the other personality.

My first disturbances were not visual at all, but concerned the more abstract matters which I have mentioned. There was, too, a feeling of profound and inexplicable horror concerning *myself.* I developed a queer fear of seeing my own form, as if my eyes would find it something utterly alien and inconceivably abhorrent. When I did glance down and behold the familiar human shape in quiet grey or blue clothing I always felt a curious relief, though in order to gain this relief I had to conquer an infinite dread. I shunned mirrors as much as possible, and was always shaved at the barber's.

It was a long time before I correlated any of these disappointed feelings with the fleeting visual impressions which began to develop. The first such correlation had to do with the odd sensation of an external, artificial restraint on my memory. I felt that the snatches of sight I experienced had a profound and terrible meaning, and a frightful connexion with myself, but that some purposeful influence held me from grasping that meaning and that connexion. Then came that queerness about the element of time, and with it desperate efforts to place the fragmentary dream-glimpses in the chronological and spatial pattern.

The glimpses themselves were at first merely strange rather than horrible. I would seem to be in an enormous vaulted chamber whose lofty stone groinings were well-nigh lost in the shadows overhead. In whatever time or place the scene might be, the principle of the arch was known as fully and used as extensively as by the Romans. There were colossal round windows and high arched doors, and pedestals or tables each as tall as the height of an ordinary room. Vast shelves of dark wood lined the walls, holding what seemed to be volumes of immense size with strange hieroglyphs on their backs. The exposed stonework held curious carvings, always in curvilinear mathematical designs, and there were chiselled inscriptions in the same characters that the huge books bore. The dark granite masonry was of a monstrous megalithic type, with lines of convex-topped blocks fitting the concave-bottomed courses which rested upon them. There were no chairs, but the tops of the vast pedestals were littered with books, papers, and what seemed to be writing materials—oddly figured jars of a purplish metal, and rods with stained tips. Tall as the pedestals were, I seemed at times able to view them from above. On some of them were great globes of luminous crystal serving as lamps, and inexplicable machines formed of vitreous tubes and metal rods. The windows were glazed, and latticed with stout-looking bars. Though I dared not approach and peer out them, I could see from where I was the waving tops of singular fern-like growths. The floor was of massive octagonal flagstones, while rugs and hangings were entirely lacking.

Later I had visions of sweeping through Cyclopean corridors of stone, and up and down gigantic inclined planes of the same monstrous masonry. There were no stairs anywhere, nor was any passageway less than thirty feet wide. Some of the structures through which I floated must have towered into the sky for thousands of feet. There were multiple levels of black vaults below, and never-opened trap-doors, sealed down with metal bands and holding dim suggestions of some special peril. I seemed to be a prisoner, and horror hung broodingly over everything I saw. I felt that the mocking curvilinear hieroglyphs on the walls would blast my soul with their message were I not guarded by a merciful ignorance.

Still later my dreams included vistas from the great round windows, and from the titanic flat roof, with its curious gardens, wide barren area, and high, scalloped parapet of stone, to which the topmost of the inclined planes led. There were almost endless leagues of giant buildings, each in its garden, and ranged along paved roads fully two hundred feet wide. They differed greatly in aspect, but few were less than five hundred feet square or a thousand feet high. Many seemed so limitless that they must have had a frontage of several thousand feet, while some shot up to mountainous altitudes in the grey, steamy heavens. They seemed to be mainly of stone or concrete, and most of them embodied the oddly curvilinear type of masonry noticeable in the building that held me. Roofs were flat and garden-covered, and tended to have scalloped parapets. Sometimes there were terraces and higher levels, and wide cleared spaces amidst the gardens. The great roads held hints of motion, but in the earlier visions I could not resolve this impression into details.

In certain places I beheld enormous dark cylindrical towers which climbed far above any of the other structures. These appeared to be of a totally unique nature, and shewed signs of prodigious age and dilapidation. They were built of a bizarre type of square-cut basalt masonry, and tapered slightly toward their rounded tops. Nowhere in any of them could the least traces of windows or other apertures save huge doors be found. I noticed also some lower buildings—all crumbling with the weathering of aeons—which resembled these dark cylindrical towers in basic architecture. Around all these aberrant piles of square-cut masonry there hovered an inexplicable aura of menace and concentrated fear, like that bred by the sealed trap-doors.

The omnipresent gardens were almost terrifying in their strangeness, with bizarre and unfamiliar forms of vegetation nodding over broad paths lined with curiously carven monoliths. Abnormally vast fern-like growths predominated; some green, and some of a ghastly, fungoid pallor. Among them rose great spectral things resembling calamites, whose bamboo-like trunks towered to fabulous heights. Then there were tufted forms like fabulous cycads, and grotesque dark-green shrubs and trees of coniferous aspect. Flowers were small, colourless, and unrecognisable, blooming in geometrical beds and at large among the greenery. In a few of the terrace and roof-top gardens were larger and more vivid blossoms of almost offensive contours and seeming to suggest artificial breeding. Fungi of inconceivable size, outlines, and colours speckled the scene in patterns bespeaking some unknown but well-established horticultural tradition. In the larger gardens on the ground there seemed to be some attempt to preserve the irregularities of Nature, but on the roofs there was more selectiveness, and more evidences of the topiary art.

The skies were almost always moist and cloudy, and sometimes I would seem to witness tremendous rains. Once in a while, though, there would be glimpses of the sun—which looked abnormally large—and of the moon, whose markings held a touch of difference from the normal that I could never quite fathom. When—very rarely—the night sky was clear to any extent, I beheld constellations which were nearly beyond recognition. Known outlines were sometimes approximated, but seldom duplicated; and from the position of the few groups I could recognise, I felt I must be in the earth's southern hemisphere, near the Tropic of Capricorn. The far horizon was always steamy and indistinct, but I could see that great jungles of unknown tree-ferns, calamites, lepidodendra, and sigillaria lay outside the city, their fantastic frondage waving mockingly in the shifting vapours. Now and then there would be suggestions of motion in the sky, but these my early visions never resolved.

By the autumn of 1914 I began to have infrequent dreams of strange floatings over the city and and through the regions around it. I saw interminable roads through forests of fearsome growths with mottled, fluted, and banded trunks, and past other cities as strange as the one which persistently haunted me. I saw monstrous constructions of black or iridescent stone in glades and clearings where perpetual twilight reigned, and traversed long causeways over swamps so dark that I could tell but little of their moist, towering vegetation. Once I saw an area of countless miles strown with age-blasted basaltic ruins whose architecture had been like that of the few windowless, round-topped towers in the haunting city. And once I saw the sea—a boundless steamy expanse beyond the colossal stone piers of an enormous town of domes and arches. Great shapeless suggestions of shadow moved over it, and here and there its surface was vexed with anomalous spoutings.

III

As I have said, it was not immediately that these wild visions began to hold their terrifying quality. Certainly, many persons have dreamed intrinsically stranger things—things compounded of unrelated scraps of daily life, pictures, and reading, and arranged in fantastically novel forms by the unchecked caprices of sleep. For some time I accepted the visions as natural, even though I had never before been an extravagant dreamer. Many of the vague anomalies, I argued, must have come from trivial sources too numerous to track down; while others seemed to reflect a common text-book knowledge of the plants and other conditions of the primitive world of a hundred and fifty million years ago—the world of the Permian or Triassic age. In the course of some months, however, the element of terror did figure with accumulating force. This was when the dreams began so unfailingly to have the aspect of memories, and when my mind began to link them with my growing abstract disturbances—the feeling of mnemonic restraint, the curious impressions regarding *time,* the sense of a loathsome exchange with my secondary personality of 1908–13, and, considerably later, the inexplicable loathing of my own person.

As certain definite details began to enter the dreams, their horror increased a thousandfold—until by October, 1915, I felt I must do something. It was then that I began an intensive study of other cases of amnesia and visions, feeling that I might thereby objectivise my trouble and shake clear of its emotional grip. However, as before mentioned, the result was at first almost exactly opposite. It disturbed me vastly to find that my dreams had been so closely duplicated; especially since some of the accounts were too early to admit of any geological knowledge—and therefore of any idea of primitive landscapes—on the subjects' part. What is more, many of these accounts supplied very horrible details and explanations in connexion with the visions of great buildings and jungle gardens—and other things. The actual sights and vague impressions were bad enough, but what was hinted or asserted by some of the other dreamers savoured of madness and blasphemy. Worst of all, my own pseudo-memory was aroused to wilder dreams and hints of coming revelations. And yet most doctors deemed my course, on the whole, an advisable one.

I studied psychology systematically, and under the prevailing stimulus my son Wingate did the same—his studies leading eventually to his present professorship. In 1917 and 1918 I took special courses at Miskatonic. Meanwhile my examination of medical, historical, and anthropological records became indefatigable; involving travels to distant libraries, and finally including even a reading of the hideous books of forbidden elder lore in which my secondary personality had been so disturbingly interested. Some of the latter were the actual copies I had consulted in my altered state, and I was greatly disturbed by certain marginal notations and ostensible *corrections* of the hideous text in a script and idiom which somehow seemed oddly unhuman.

These markings were mostly in the respective languages of the various books, all of which the writer seemed to know with equal though obviously academic facility. One note appended to von Junzt's

Unaussprechlichen Kulten, however, was alarmingly otherwise. It consisted of certain curvilinear hieroglyphs in the same ink as that of the German corrections, but following no recognised human pattern. And these hieroglyphs were closely and unmistakably akin to the characters constantly met with in my dreams—characters whose meaning I would sometimes momentarily fancy I knew or was just on the brink of recalling. To complete my black confusion, many librarians assured me that, in view of previous examinations and records of consultation of the volumes in question, all of these notations must have been made by myself in my secondary state. This despite the fact that I was and still am ignorant of three of the languages involved.

Piecing together the scattered records, ancient and modern, anthropological and medical, I found a fairly consistent mixture of myth and hallucination whose scope and wildness left me utterly dazed. Only one thing consoled me—the fact that the myths were of such early existence. What lost knowledge could have brought pictures of the Palaeozoic or Mesozoic landscape into these primitive fables, I could not even guess, but the pictures had been there. Thus, a basis existed for the formation of a fixed type of delusion. Cases of amnesia no doubt created the general myth-pattern—but afterward the fanciful accretions of the myths must have reacted on amnesia sufferers and coloured their pseudo-memories. I myself had read and heard all the early tales during my memory lapse—my quest had amply proved that. Was it not natural, then, for my subsequent dreams and emotional impressions to become coloured and moulded by what my memory subtly held over from my secondary state? A few of the myths had significant connexions with other cloudy legends of the pre-human world, especially those Hindoo tales involving stupefying gulfs of time and forming part of the lore of modern theosophists.

Primal myth and modern delusion joined in their assumption that mankind is only one—perhaps the least—of the highly evolved and dominant races of this planet's long and largely unknown career. Things of inconceivable shape, they implied, had reared towers to the sky and delved into every secret of Nature before the first amphibian forbear of man had crawled out of the hot sea three hundred million years ago. Some had come down from the stars; a few were as old as the cosmos itself; others had arisen swiftly from terrene germs as far behind the first germs of our life-cycle as those germs are behind ourselves. Spans of thousands of millions of years, and linkages with other galaxies and universes, were freely spoken of. Indeed, there was no such thing as time in its humanly accepted sense.

But most of the tales and impressions concerned a relatively late race, of a queer and intricate shape resembling no life-form known to science, which had lived till only fifty million years before the advent of man. This, they indicated, was the greatest race of all; because it alone had conquered the secret of time. It had learned all things that ever were known *or ever would be known* on the earth, through the power of its keener minds to project themselves into the past and future, even through gulfs of millions of years, and study the lore of every age. From the accomplishments of this race arose all legends of *prophets*, including those in human mythology.

In its vast libraries were volumes of texts and pictures holding the whole of earth's annals—histories and descriptions of every species that had ever been or that ever would be, with full records of their arts, their achievements, their languages, and their psychologies. With this aeon-embracing knowledge, the Great Race chose from every era and life-form such thoughts, arts, and processes as might suit its own nature and situation. Knowledge of the past, secured through a kind of mind-casting outside the recognised senses, was harder to glean than knowledge of the future.

In the latter case the course was easier and more material. With suitable mechanical aid a mind would project itself forward in time, feeling its dim, extra-sensory way till it approached the desired period. Then, after preliminary trials, it would seize on the best discoverable representative of the highest of that period's life-forms; entering the organism's brain and setting up therein its own vibrations while the displaced mind would strike back to the period of the displacer, remaining in the latter's body till a reverse process was set up. The projected mind, in the body of the organism of the future, would then pose as a member of the race whose outward form it wore; learning as quickly as possible all that could be learned of the chosen age and its massed information and techniques.

Meanwhile the displaced mind, thrown back to the displacer's age and body, would be carefully guarded. It would be kept from harming the body it occupied, and would be drained of all its knowledge by trained questioners. Often it could be questioned in its own language, when previous quests into the future had brought back records of that language. If the mind came from a body whose language the Great Race could not physically reproduce, clever machines would be made, on which the alien speech could be played as on a musical instrument. The Great Race's members were immense rugose cones ten feet high, and with head and other organs attached to foot-thick, distensible limbs spreading from the apexes. They spoke by the clicking or scraping of huge paws or claws attached to the end of two of their four limbs, and walked by the expansion and contraction of a viscous layer attached to their vast ten-foot bases.

When the captive mind's amazement and resentment had worn off, and when (assuming that it came from a body vastly different from the Great Race's) it had lost its horror at its unfamiliar temporary form, it was permitted to study its new environment and experience a wonder and wisdom approximating that of its displacer. With suitable precautions, and in exchange for suitable services, it was allowed to rove all over the habitable world in titan airships or on the huge boat-like atomic-engined vehicles which traversed the great roads, and to delve freely into the libraries containing the records of the planet's past and future. This reconciled many captive minds to their lot; since none were other than keen, and to such minds the unveiling of hidden mysteries of earth—closed chapters of inconceivable pasts and dizzying vortices of future time which include the years ahead of their own natural ages—forms always, despite the abysmal horrors often unveiled, the supreme experience of life.

Now and then certain captives were permitted to meet other captive minds seized from the future—to exchange thoughts with consciousnesses living a hundred or a thousand or a million years before or after their own ages. And all were urged to write copiously in their own languages of themselves and their respective periods; such documents to be filed in the great central archives.

It may be added that there was one sad special type of captive whose privileges were far greater than those of the majority. These were the dying *permanent* exiles, whose bodies in the future had been seized by keen-minded members of the Great Race who, faced with death, sought to escape mental extinction. Such melancholy exiles were not as common as might be expected, since the longevity of the Great Race lessened its love of life—especially among those superior minds capable of projection. From cases of the permanent projection of elder minds arose many of those lasting changes of personality noticed in later history—including mankind's.

As for the ordinary cases of exploration—when the displacing mind had learned what it wished in the future, it would build an apparatus like that which had started its flight and reverse the process of projection. Once more it would be in its own body in its own age, while the lately captive mind would return to that body of the future to which it properly belonged. Only when one or the other of the bodies had died during the exchange was this restoration impossible. In such cases, of course, the exploring mind had—like those of the death-escapers—to live out an alien-bodied life in the future; or else the captive mind—like the dying permanent exiles—had to end its days in the form and past age of the Great Race.

This fate was least horrible when the captive mind was also of the Great Race—a not infrequent occurrence, since in all its periods that race was intensely concerned with its own future. The number of dying permanent exiles of the Great Race was very slight—largely because of the tremendous penalties attached to displacements of future Great Race minds by the moribund. Through projection, arrangements were made to inflict these penalties on the offending minds in their new future bodies—and sometimes forced re-exchanges were effected. Complex cases of the displacement of exploring or already captive minds by minds in various regions of the past had been known and carefully rectified. In every age since the discovery of mind-projection, a minute but well-recognised element of the population consisted of Great Race minds from past ages, sojourning for a longer or shorter while.

When a captive mind of alien origin was returned to its own body in the future, it was purged by an intricate mechanical hypnosis of all it had learned in the Great Race's age—this because of certain troublesome consequences inherent in the general carrying forward of knowledge in large quantities. The few existing instances of clear transmission had caused, and would cause at known future times, great disasters. And it was largely in consequence of two cases of the kind (said the old myths) that mankind had learned what it had concerning the Great Race. Of all things surviving *physically and directly* from that aeon-distant world, there remained only certain ruins of great stones in far places and under the sea, and parts of the text of the frightful Pnakotic Manuscripts.

Thus the returning mind reached its own age with only the faintest and most fragmentary visions of what it had undergone since its seizure. All memories that could be eradicated were eradicated, so that in most cases only a dream-shadowed blank stretched back to the time of the first exchange. Some minds recalled more than others, and the chance joining of memories had at rare times brought hints of the forbidden past to future ages. There probably never was a time when groups or cults did not secretly cherish certain of these hints. In the *Necronomicon* the presence of such a cult among human beings was suggested—a cult that sometimes gave aid to minds voyaging down the aeons from the days of the Great Race.

And meanwhile the Great Race itself waxed well-nigh omniscient, and turned to the task of setting up exchanges with the minds of other planets, and of exploring their pasts and futures. It sought likewise to fathom the past years and origin of that black, aeon-dead orb in far space whence its own mental heritage had come—for the mind of the Great Race was older than its bodily form. The beings of a dying elder world, wise with the ultimate secrets, had looked ahead for a new world and species wherein they might have long life; and had sent their minds en masse into that future race best adapted to house them—the cone-shaped things that peopled our earth a billion years ago. Thus the Great Race came to be, while the myriad minds sent backward were left to die in the horror of strange shapes. Later the race would again face death, yet would live through another forward migration of its best minds into the bodies of others who had a longer physical span ahead of them.

Such was the background of intertwined legend and hallucination. When, around 1920, I had my researches in coherent shape, I felt a slight lessening of the tension which their earlier stages had increased. After all, and in spite of the fancies prompted by blind emotions, were not most of my phenomena readily explainable? Any chance might have turned my mind to dark studies during the amnesia—and then I read the forbidden legends and met the members of ancient and ill-regarded cults. That, plainly, supplied the material for the dreams and disturbed feelings which came after the return of memory. As for the marginal notes in dream-hieroglyphs and languages unknown to me, but laid at my door by librarians—I might easily have picked up a smattering of the tongues during my secondary state, while the hieroglyphs were doubtless coined by my fancy from descriptions in old legends, and *afterward* woven into my dreams. I tried to verify certain points through conversation with known cult-leaders, but never succeeded in establishing the right connexions.

At times the parallelism of so many cases in so many distant ages continued to worry me as it had at first, but on the other hand I reflected that the excitant folklore was undoubtedly more universal in the past than in the present. Probably all the other victims whose cases were like mine had had a long and familiar knowledge of the tales I had learned only when in my secondary state. When these victims had lost their memory, they had associated themselves with the creatures of their household myths—the fabulous invaders supposed to displace men's minds—and had thus embarked upon quests for knowledge which they thought they could take back to a fancied, non-human past. Then when their memory returned, they reversed the associative process and thought of themselves as the former captive minds instead of as the displacers. Hence the dreams and pseudo-memories following the conventional myth-pattern.

Despite the seeming cumbrousness of these explanations, they came finally to supersede all others in my mind—largely because of the greater weakness of any rival theory. And a substantial number of eminent psychologists and anthropologists gradually agreed with me. The more I reflected, the more convincing did my reasoning seem; till in the end I had a really effective bulwark against the visions and impressions which still assailed me. Suppose I did see strange things at night? These were only what I had heard and read of. Suppose I did have odd loathings and perspectives and pseudo-memories? These, too, were only echoes of myths absorbed in my secondary state. Nothing that I might dream, nothing that I might feel, could be of any actual significance.

Fortified by this philosophy, I greatly improved in nervous equilibrium, even though the visions (rather than the abstract impressions) steadily became more frequent and more disturbingly detailed. In 1922 I felt able to undertake regular work again, and put my newly gained knowledge to practical use by accepting an instructorship in psychology at the university. My old chair of political economy had long been adequately filled—besides which, methods of teaching economics had changed greatly since my heyday. My son was at this time just entering on the post-graduate studies leading to his present professorship, and we worked together a great deal.

IV

I continued, however, to keep a careful record of the outré, dreams which crowded upon me so thickly and vividly. Such a record, I argued, was of genuine value as a psychological document. The glimpses still seemed damnably like *memories*, though I fought off this impression with a goodly measure of success. In writing, I treated the phantasmata as things seen; but at all other times I brushed them aside like any gossamer illusions of the night. I had never mentioned such matters in common conversation; though reports of them, filtering out as such things will, had aroused sundry rumours regarding my mental health. It is amusing to reflect that these rumours were confined wholly to laymen, without a single champion among physicians or psychologists.

Of my visions after 1914 I will here mention only a few, since fuller accounts and records are at the disposal of the serious student. It is evident that with time the curious inhibitions somewhat waned, for the scope of my visions vastly increased. They have never, though, become other than disjointed fragments seemingly without clear motivation. Within the dreams I seemed gradually to acquire a greater and greater freedom of wandering. I floated through many strange buildings of stone, going from one to the other along mammoth underground passages which seemed to form the common avenues of transit. Sometimes I encountered those gigantic sealed trap-doors in the lowest level, around which such an aura of fear and forbiddenness clung. I saw tremendous tessellated pools, and rooms of curious and inexplicable utensils of myriad sorts. Then there were colossal caverns of intricate machinery whose outlines and purpose were wholly strange to me, and whose *sound* manifested itself only after many years of dreaming. I may here remark that sight and sound are the only senses I have ever exercised in the visionary world.

The real horror began in May, 1915, when I first saw the *living things*. This was before my studies had taught me what, in view of the myths and case histories, to expect. As mental barriers wore down, I beheld great masses of thin vapour in various parts of the building and in the streets below. These steadily grew more solid and distinct, till at last I could trace their monstrous outlines with uncomfortable ease. They seemed to be enormous iridescent cones, about ten feet high and ten feet wide at the base, and made up of some ridgy, scaly, semi-elastic matter. From their apexes projected four flexible, cylindrical members, each a foot thick, and of a ridgy substance like that of the cones themselves. These members were sometimes contracted almost to nothing, and sometimes extended to any distance up to about ten feet. Terminating two of them were enormous claws or nippers. At the end of a third were four red, trumpet-like appendages. The fourth terminated in an irregular yellowish globe some two feet in diameter and having three great dark eyes ranged along its central circumference. Surmounting this head were four slender grey stalks bearing flower-like appendages, whilst from its nether side dangled eight greenish antennae or tentacles. The great base of the central cone was fringed with a rubbery, grey substance which moved the whole entity through expansion and contraction.

The real horror began in May, 1915, when I first saw the living things.

Their actions, though harmless, horrified me even more than their appearance—for it is not wholesome to watch monstrous objects doing what one has known only human beings to do. These objects moved intelligently around the great rooms, getting books from the shelves and taking them to the great tables, or vice versa, and sometimes writing diligently with a peculiar rod gripped in the greenish head-tentacles. The huge nippers were used in carrying books and in conversation—speech consisting of a kind of clicking and scraping. The objects had no clothing, but wore satchels or knap-sacks suspended from the top of the conical trunk. They commonly carried their head and its supporting member at the level of the cone top, although it was frequently raised or lowered. The other three great members tended to rest downward on the sides of the cone, contracted to about five feet each, when not in use. From their rate of reading, writing, and operating their machines (those on the tables seemed somehow connected with thought) I concluded that their intelligence was enormously greater than man's.

Afterward I saw them everywhere; swarming in all the great chambers and corridors, tending monstrous machines in vaulted crypts, and racing along the vast roads in gigantic boat-shaped cars. I ceased to be afraid of them, for they seemed to form supremely natural parts of their environment. Individual differences amongst them began to be manifest, and a few appeared to be under some kind of restraint. These latter, though shewing no physical variation, had a diversity of gestures and habits which marked them off not only from the majority, but very largely from one another. They wrote a great deal in what seemed to my cloudy vision a vast variety of characters— never the typical curvilinear hieroglyphs of the majority. A few, I fancied, used our own familiar alphabet. Most of them worked much more slowly than the general mass of the entities.

All this time *my own part* in the dreams seemed to be that of a disembodied consciousness with a range of vision wider than the normal; floating freely about, yet confined to the ordinary avenues and speeds of travel. Not until August, 1915, did any suggestions of bodily existence begin to harass me. I say *harass*, because the first phase was a purely abstract though infinitely terrible association of my previously noted body-loathing with the scenes of my visions. For a while my chief concern during dreams was to avoid looking down at myself, and I recall how grateful I was for the total absence of large mirrors in the strange rooms. I was mightily troubled by the fact that I always saw the great tables—whose height could not be under ten feet—from a level not below that of their surfaces.

And then the morbid temptation to look down at myself became greater and greater, till one night I could not resist it. At first my downward glance revealed nothing whatever. A moment later I perceived that this was because my head lay at the end of a flexible neck of enormous length. Retracting this neck and gazing down very sharply, I saw the scaly, rugose, iridescent bulk of a vast cone ten feet tall and ten feet wide at the base. That was when I waked half of Arkham with my screaming as I plunged madly up from the abyss of sleep.

Only after weeks of hideous repetition did I grow half-reconciled to these visions of myself in monstrous form. In the dreams I now moved bodily among the other unknown entities, reading terrible books from the endless shelves and writing for hours at the great tables with a stylus managed by the green tentacles that hung down from my head. Snatches of what I read and wrote would linger in my memory. There were horrible annals of other worlds and other universes, and of stirrings of formless life outside of all universes. There were records of strange orders of beings which had peopled the world in forgotten pasts, and frightful chronicles of grotesque-bodied intelligences which would people it millions of years after the death of the last human being. And I learned of chapters in human history whose existence no scholar of today has ever suspected. Most of these writings were in the language of the hieroglyphs; which I studied in a queer way with the aid of droning machines, and which was evidently an agglutinative speech with root systems utterly unlike any found in human languages. Other volumes were in other unknown tongues learned in the same queer way. A very few were in languages I knew. Extremely clever pictures, both inserted in the records and forming separate collections, aided me immensely. And all the time I seemed to be setting down a history of my own age in English. On waking, I could recall only minute and meaningless scraps of the unknown tongues which my dream-self had mastered, though whole phrases of the history stayed with me.

I learned—even before my waking self had studied the parallel cases or the old myths from which the dreams doubtless sprang—that the entities around me were of the world's greatest race, which had conquered time and had sent exploring minds into every age. I knew, too, that I had been snatched from my age while *another* used my body in that age, and that a few of the other strange forms housed similarly captured minds. I seemed to talk, in some odd language of claw-clickings, with exiled intellects from every corner of the solar system.

There was a mind from the planet we know as Venus, which would live incalculable epochs to come, and one from an outer moon of Jupiter six million years in the past. Of earthly minds there were some from the winged, star-headed, half-vegetable race of palaeogean Antarctica; one from the reptile people of fabled Valusia; three from the furry pre-human Hyperborean worshippers of Tsathoggua; one from the wholly abominable Tcho-Tchos; two from the arachnid denizens of earth's last age; five from the hardy coleopterous species immediately following mankind, to which the Great Race was some day to transfer its keenest minds en masse in the face of horrible peril; and several from different branches of humanity.

I talked with the mind of Yiang-Li, a philosopher from the cruel empire of Tsan-Chan, which is to come in A.D. 5000; with that of a general of the great-headed brown people who held South Africa in B.C. 50,000; with that of a twelfth-century Florentine monk named Bartolomeo Corsi; with that of a king of Lomar who had ruled that terrible polar land 100,000 years before the squat, yellow Inutos came from the west to engulf it; with that of Nug-Soth, a magician of the dark conquerors of A.D. 16,000; with that of a Roman named

Titus Sempronius Blaesus, who had been a quaestor in Sulla's time; with that of Khephnes, an Egyptian of the 14th Dynasty who told me the hideous secret of Nyarlathotep; with that of a priest of Atlantis' middle kingdom; with that of a Suffolk gentleman of Cromwell's day, James Woodville; with that of a court astronomer of pre-Inca Peru; with that of the Australian physicist Nevil Kingston-Brown, who will die in A.D. 2518; with that of an archimage of vanished Yhe in the Pacific; with that of Theodotides, a Graeco-Bactrian official of B.C. 200; with that of an aged Frenchman of Louis XIII's time named Pierre-Louis Montmagny; with that of Crom-Ya, a Cimmerian chieftain of B.C. 15,000; and with so many others that my brain cannot hold the shocking secrets and dizzying marvels I learned from them.

I awaked each morning in a fever, sometimes frantically trying to verify or discredit such information as fell within the range of modern human knowledge. Traditional facts took on new and doubtful aspects, and I marvelled at the dream-fancy which could invent such surprising addenda to history and science. I shivered at the mysteries the past may conceal, and trembled at the menaces the future may bring forth. What was hinted in the speech of post-human entities of the fate of mankind produced such an effect on me that I will not set it down here. After man there would be the mighty beetle civilisation, the bodies of whose members the cream of the Great Race would seize when the monstrous doom overtook the elder world. Later, as the earth's span closed, the transferred minds would again migrate through time and space—to another stopping-place in the bodies of the bulbous vegetable entities of Mercury. But there would be races after them, clinging pathetically to the cold planet and burrowing to its horror-filled core, before the utter end.

Meanwhile, in my dreams, I wrote endlessly in that history of my own age which I was preparing—half voluntarily and half through promises of increased library and travel opportunities—for the Great Race's central archives. The archives were in a colossal subterranean structure near the city's centre, which I came to know well through

I seemed to talk, in some odd language of claw-clickings . . .

... with exiled intellects from every corner of the solar system.

37

frequent labours and consultations. Meant to last as long as the race, and to withstand the fiercest of earth's convulsions, this titan repository surpassed all other buildings in the massive, mountain-like firmness of its construction.

The records, written or printed on great sheets of a curiously tenacious cellulose fabric, were bound into books that opened from the top, and were kept in individual cases of a strange, extremely light rustless metal of greyish hue, decorated with mathematical designs and bearing the title in the Great Race's curvilinear hieroglyphs. These cases were stored in tiers of rectangular vaults—like closed, locked shelves—wrought of the same rustless metal and fastened by knobs with intricate turnings. My own history was assigned a specific place in the vaults of the lowest or vertebrate level—the section devoted to the culture of mankind and of the furry and reptilian races immediately preceding it in terrestrial dominance.

But none of the dreams ever gave me a full picture of daily life. All were the merest misty, disconnected fragments, and it is certain that these fragments were not unfolded in their rightful sequence. I have, for example, a very imperfect idea of my own living arrangements in the dream-world; though I seem to have possessed a great stone room of my own. My restrictions as a prisoner gradually disappeared, so that some of the visions included vivid travels over the mighty jungle roads, sojourns in strange cities, and explorations of some of the vast dark windowless ruins from which the Great Race shrank in curious fear. There were also long sea-voyages in enormous, many-decked boats of incredible swiftness, and trips over wild regions in closed, projectile-like airships lifted and moved by electrical repulsion. Beyond the wide, warm ocean were other cities of the Great Race, and on one far continent I saw the crude villages of the black-snouted, winged creatures who would evolve as a dominant stock after the Great Race had sent its foremost minds into the future to escape the creeping horror. Flatness and exuberant green life were always the keynote of the scene. Hills were low and sparse, and usually displayed signs of volcanic forces.

Of the animals I saw, I could write volumes.

Of the animals I saw, I could write volumes. All were wild; for the Great Race's mechanised culture had long since done away with domestic beasts, while food was wholly vegetable or synthetic. Clumsy reptiles of great bulk floundered in steaming morasses, fluttered in the heavy air, or spouted in the seas and lakes; and among these I fancied I could vaguely recognise lesser, archaic prototypes of many forms—dinosaurs, pterodactyls, ichthyosaurs, labyrinthodonts, rhamphorhynci, plesiosaurs, and the like—made familiar through palaeontology. Of birds or mammals there were none that I could discern.

The ground and swamps were constantly alive with snakes, lizards, and crocodiles, while insects buzzed incessantly amidst the lush vegetation. And far out at sea unspied and unknown monsters spouted mountainous columns of foam into the vaporous sky. Once I was taken under the ocean in a gigantic submarine vessel with searchlights, and glimpsed some living horrors of awesome magnitude. I saw also the ruins of incredible sunken cities, and the wealth of crinoid, brachiopod, coral, and ichthyic life which everywhere abounded.

Of the physiology, psychology, folkways, and detailed history of the Great Race my visions preserved but little information, and many of the scattered points I here set down were gleaned from my study of old legends and other cases rather than from my own dreaming. For in time, of course, my reading and research caught up with and passed the dreams in many phases; so that certain dream-fragments were explained in advance, and formed verifications of what I had learned. This consolingly established my belief that similar reading and research, accomplished by my secondary self, had formed the source of the whole terrible fabric of pseudo-memories.

The period of my dreams, apparently, was one somewhat less than 150,000,000 years ago, when the Palaeozoic age was giving place to the Mesozoic. The bodies occupied by the Great Race represented no surviving—or even scientifically known—line of terrestrial evolution, but were of a peculiar, closely homogeneous, and highly specialised organic type inclining as much to the vegetable as to the animal state. Cell-action was of an unique sort almost precluding fatigue, and wholly eliminating the need of sleep. Nourishment, assimilated through the red trumpet-like appendages on one of the great flexible limbs, was always semi-fluid and in many aspects wholly unlike the food of existing animals. The beings had but two of the senses which we recognise—sight and hearing, the latter accomplished through the flower-like appendages on the grey stalks above their heads—but of other and incomprehensible senses (not, however, well utilisable by alien captive minds inhabiting their bodies) they possessed many. Their three eyes were so situated as to give them a range of vision wider than the normal. Their blood was a sort of deep-greenish ichor of great thickness. They had no sex, but reproduced through seeds or spores which clustered on their bases and could be developed only under water. Great, shallow tanks were used for the growth of their young—which were, however, reared only in small numbers on account of the longevity of individuals; four or five thousand years being the common life span.

Markedly defective individuals were quietly disposed of as soon as their defects were noticed. Disease and the approach of death were, in the absence of a sense of touch or of physical pain, recognised by purely visual symptoms. The dead were incinerated with dignified ceremonies. Once in a while, as before mentioned, a keen mind would escape death by forward projection in time; but such cases were not numerous. When one did occur, the exiled mind from the future was treated with the utmost kindness till the dissolution of its unfamiliar tenement.

The Great Race seemed to form a single loosely knit nation or league, with major institutions in common, though there were four definite divisions. The political and economic system of each unit was a sort of fascistic socialism, with major resources rationally distributed, and power delegated to a small governing board elected by the votes of all able to pass certain educational and psychological tests. Family organisation was not overstressed, though ties among persons of common descent were recognised, and the young were generally reared by their parents.

Once I was taken under the ocean in a gigantic submarine vessel with searchlights . . .

. . . and glimpsed some living horrors of awesome magnitude.

The Great Race seemed to form a single loosely knit nation or league . . .

. . . with major institutions in common, though there were four definite divisions.

Resemblances to human attitudes and institutions were, of course, most marked in those fields where on the one hand highly abstract elements were concerned, or where on the other hand there was a dominance of the basic, unspecialised urges common to all organic life. A few added likenesses came through conscious adoption as the Great Race probed the future and copied what it liked. Industry, highly mechanised, demanded but little time from each citizen; and the abundant leisure was filled with intellectual and aesthetic activities of various sorts. The sciences were carried to an unbelievable height of development, and art was a vital part of life, though at the period of my dreams it had passed its crest and meridian. Technology was enormously stimulated through the constant struggle to survive, and to keep in existence the physical fabric of great cities, imposed by the prodigious geologic upheavals of those primal days.

Crime was surprisingly scanty, and was dealt with through highly efficient policing. Punishments ranged from privilege-deprivation and imprisonment to death or major emotion-wrenching, and were never administered without a careful study of the criminal's motivations. Warfare, largely civil for the last few millennia though sometimes waged against reptilian and octopodic invaders, or against the winged, star-headed Old Ones who centred in the Antarctic, was infrequent though infinitely devastating. An enormous army, using camera-like weapons which produced tremendous electrical effects, was kept on hand for purposes seldom mentioned, but obviously connected with the ceaseless fear of the dark, windowless elder ruins and of the great sealed trap-doors in the lowest subterrene levels.

This fear of the basalt ruins and trap-doors was largely a matter of unspoken suggestion—or, at most, of furtive quasi-whispers. Everything specific which bore on it was significantly absent from such books as were on the common shelves. It was the one subject lying altogether under a taboo among the Great Race, and seemed to be connected alike with horrible bygone struggles, and with that future peril which would some day force the race to send its keener minds ahead en masse in time. Imperfect and fragmentary as were the other things presented by dreams and legends, this matter was still more bafflingly shrouded. The vague old myths avoided it—or perhaps all allusions had for some reason been excised. And in the dreams of myself and others, the hints were peculiarly few. Members of the Great Race never intentionally referred to the matter, and what could be gleaned came only from some of the more sharply observant captive minds.

According to these scraps of information, the basis of the fear was a horrible elder race of half-polypous, utterly alien entities which had come through space from immeasurably distant universes and had dominated the earth and three other solar planets about six hundred million years ago. They were only partly material—as we understand matter—and their type of consciousness and media of perception differed wholly from those of terrestrial organisms. For example, their senses did not include that of sight; their mental world being a strange, non-visual pattern of impressions. They were, however, sufficiently material to use implements of normal matter when in cosmic areas containing it; and they required housing—albeit of a peculiar kind. Though their *senses* could penetrate all material barriers, their *substance* could not; and certain forms of electrical energy could wholly destroy them. They had the power of aërial motion despite the absence of wings or any other visible means of levitation. Their minds were of such texture that no exchange with them could be effected by the Great Race.

When these things had come to the earth they had built mighty basalt cities of windowless towers, and had preyed horribly upon the beings they found. Thus it was when the minds of the Great Race sped across the void from that obscure trans-galactic world known in the disturbing and debatable Eltdown Shards as Yith. The newcomers, with the instruments they created, had found it easy to subdue the predatory entities and drive them down to those caverns of inner earth which they had already joined to their abodes and begun to inhabit. Then they had sealed the entrances and left them to their fate, afterward occupying most of their great cities and preserving certain important buildings for reasons connected more with superstition than with indifference, boldness, or scientific and historical zeal.

But as the aeons passed, there came vague, evil signs that the Elder Things were growing strong and numerous in the inner world. There were sporadic irruptions of a particularly hideous character in certain small and remote cities of the Great Race, and in some of the deserted elder cities which the Great Race had not peopled—places where the paths to the gulfs below had not been properly sealed or guarded. After that greater precautions were taken, and many of the paths were closed for ever—though a few were left with sealed trap-doors for strategic use in fighting the Elder Things if ever they broke forth in unexpected places; fresh rifts caused by that selfsame geologic change which had choked some of the paths and had slowly lessened the number of outer-world structures and ruins surviving from the conquered entities.

The irruptions of the Elder Things must have been shocking beyond all description, since they had permanently coloured the psychology of the Great Race. Such was the fixed mood of horror that the very aspect of the creatures was left unmentioned—at no time was I able to gain a clear hint of what they looked like. There were veiled suggestions of a monstrous *plasticity*, and of temporary *lapses of visibility*, while other fragmentary whispers referred to their control and military use of *great winds*. Singular *whistling* noises, and colossal footprints made up of five circular toe-marks, seemed also to be associated with them.

It was evident that the coming doom so desperately feared by the Great Race—the doom that was one day to send millions of keen minds across the chasm of time to strange bodies in the safer future—had to do with a final successful irruption of the Elder Beings. Mental projections down the ages had clearly foretold such a horror, and the Great Race had resolved that none who could escape should face it. That the foray would be a matter of vengeance, rather than an attempt to reoccupy the outer world, they knew from the planet's later history—for their projections shewed the coming

and going of subsequent races untroubled by the monstrous entities. Perhaps these entities had come to prefer earth's inner abysses
to the variable, storm-ravaged surface, since light meant nothing
to them. Perhaps, too, they were slowly weakening with the aeons.
Indeed, it was known that they would be quite dead in the time of
the post-human beetle race which the fleeing minds would tenant.
Meanwhile the Great Race maintained its cautious vigilance, with
potent weapons ceaselessly ready despite the horrified banishing of
the subject from common speech and visible records. And always the
shadow of nameless fear hung about the sealed trap-doors and the
dark, windowless elder towers.

The irruptions of the Elder Things must have been shocking beyond all description . . .

. . . since they had permanently coloured the psychology of the Great Race.

V

That is the world of which my dreams brought me dim, scattered echoes every night. I cannot hope to give any true idea of the horror and dread contained in such echoes, for it was upon a wholly intangible quality—the sharp sense of *pseudo-memory*—that such feelings mainly depended. As I have said, my studies gradually gave me a defence against these feelings, in the form of rational psychological explanations; and this saving influence was augmented by the subtle touch of accustomedness which comes with the passage of time. Yet in spite of everything the vague, creeping terror would return momentarily now and then. It did not, however, engulf me as it had before; and after 1922 I lived a very normal life of work and recreation.

In the course of years I began to feel that my experience—together with the kindred cases and the related folklore—ought to be definitely summarised and published for the benefit of serious students; hence I prepared a series of articles briefly covering the whole ground and illustrated with crude sketches of some of the shapes, scenes, decorative motifs, and hieroglyphs remembered from the dreams. These appeared at various times during 1928 and 1929 in the *Journal of the American Psychological Society*, but did not attract much attention. Meanwhile I continued to record my dreams with the minutest care, even though the growing stack of reports attained troublesomely vast proportions.

On July 10, 1934, there was forwarded to me by the Psychological Society the letter which opened the culminating and most horrible phase of the whole mad ordeal. It was postmarked Pilbarra, Western Australia, and bore the signature of one whom I found, upon inquiry, to be a mining engineer of considerable prominence. Enclosed were some very curious snapshots. I will reproduce the text in its entirety, and no reader can fail to understand how tremendous an effect it and the photographs had upon me.

I was, for a time, almost stunned and incredulous; for although I had often thought that some basis of fact must underlie certain phases of the legends which had coloured my dreams, I was none the less unprepared for anything like a tangible survival from a lost world remote beyond all imagination. Most devastating of all were the photographs—for here, in cold, incontrovertible realism, there stood out against a background of sand certain worn-down, water-ridged, storm-weathered blocks of stone whose slightly convex tops and slightly concave bottoms told their own story. And when I studied them with a magnifying glass I could see all too plainly, amidst the batterings and pittings, the traces of those vast curvilinear designs and occasional hieroglyphs whose significance had become so hideous to me. But here is the letter, which speaks for itself:

> 49, Dampier Str.,
> Pilbarra, W. Australia,
> 18 May, 1934.

Prof. N. W. Peaslee,
c/o Am. Psychological Society,
30, E. 41st Str.,
N. Y. City, U.S.A.

My dear Sir:—

A recent conversation with Dr. E. M. Boyle of Perth, and some papers with your articles which he has just sent me, make it advisable for me to tell you about certain things I have seen in the Great Sandy Desert east of our gold field here. It would seem, in view of the peculiar legends about old cities with huge stonework and strange designs and hieroglyphs which you describe, that I have come upon something very important.

The blackfellows have always been full of talk about "great stones with marks on them", and seem to have a terrible fear of such things. They connect them in some way with their common racial legends about Buddai, the gigantic old man who lies asleep for ages underground with his head on his arm, and who will some day awake and eat up the world. There are some very old and half-forgotten tales of enormous underground huts of great stones, where passages lead down and down, and where horrible things have happened. The blackfellows claim that once some warriors, fleeing in battle, went down into one and never came back, but that frightful winds began to blow from the place soon after they went down. However, there usually isn't much in what these natives say.

But what I have to tell is more than this. Two years ago, when I was prospecting about 500 miles east in the desert, I came on a lot of queer pieces of dressed stone perhaps 3 × 2 × 2 feet in size, and weathered and pitted to the very limit. At first I couldn't find any of the marks the blackfellows told about, but when I looked close enough I could make out some deeply carved lines in spite of the weathering. They were peculiar curves, just like what the blacks had tried to describe. I imagine there must have been 30 or 40 blocks, some nearly buried in the sand, and all within a circle perhaps a quarter of a mile's diameter.

When I saw some, I looked around closely for more, and made a careful reckoning of the place with my instruments. I also took pictures of 10 or 12 of the most typical blocks, and will enclose the prints for you to see. I turned my information and pictures over to the government at Perth, but they have done nothing with them.

Then I met Dr. Boyle, who had read your articles in the *Journal of the American Psychological Society*, and in time happened to mention the stones. He was enormously interested, and became quite excited when I shewed him my snapshots, saying that the stones and markings were just like those of the masonry you had dreamed about and seen described in legends. He meant to write you, but was delayed. Meanwhile he sent me most of the magazines with your articles, and I saw at once from your drawings and descriptions that my stones are certainly the kind you mean. You can appreciate this from the enclosed prints. Later on you will hear directly from Dr. Boyle.

Now I can understand how important all this will be to you. Without question we are faced with the remains of an unknown civilisation older than any dreamed of before, and forming a basis for your legends. As a mining engineer, I have some knowledge of geology, and can tell you that these blocks are so ancient they frighten me. They are mostly sandstone and granite, though one is almost certainly made of a queer sort of *cement* or *concrete*. They bear evidence of water action, as if this part of the world had been submerged and come up again after long ages—all since these blocks were made and used. It is a matter of hundreds of thousands of years—or heaven knows how much more. I don't like to think about it.

In view of your previous diligent work in tracking down the legends and everything connected with them, I cannot doubt but that you will want to lead an expedition to the desert and make some archaeological excavations. Both Dr. Boyle and I are prepared to coöperate in such work if you—or organisations known to you—can furnish the funds. I can get together a dozen miners for the heavy digging—the blacks would be of no use, for I've found that they have an almost maniacal fear of this particular spot. Boyle and I are saying nothing to others, for you very obviously ought to have precedence in any discoveries or credit.

The place can be reached from Pilbarra in about 4 days by motor tractor—which we'd need for our apparatus. It is somewhat west and south of Warburton's path of 1873, and 100 miles southeast of Joanna Spring. We could float things up the De Grey River instead of starting from Pilbarra—but all that can be talked over later. Roughly, the stones lie at a point about 22° 3' 14" South Latitude, 125° 0' 39" East Longitude. The climate is tropical, and the desert conditions are trying. Any expedition had better be made in winter—June or July or August. I shall welcome further correspondence upon this subject, and am keenly eager to assist in any plan you may devise. After studying your articles I am deeply impressed with the profound significance of the whole matter. Dr. Boyle will write later. When rapid communication is needed, a cable to Perth can be relayed by wireless.

Hoping profoundly for an early message
   Believe me,
     Most faithfully yours,
       Robert B. F. Mackenzie.

Of the immediate aftermath of this letter, much can be learned from the press. My good fortune in securing the backing of Miskatonic University was great, and both Mr. Mackenzie and Dr. Boyle proved invaluable in arranging matters at the Australian end. We were not too specific with the public about our objects, since the whole matter would have lent itself unpleasantly to sensational and jocose treatment by the cheaper newspapers. As a result, printed reports were sparing; but enough appeared to tell of our quest for reported Australian ruins and to chronicle our various preparatory steps.

Professors William Dyer of the college's geology department (leader of the Miskatonic Antarctic Expedition of 1930–31), Ferdinand C. Ashley of the department of ancient history, and Tyler M. Freeborn of the department of anthropology—together with my son Wingate—accompanied me. My correspondent Mackenzie came to Arkham early in 1935 and assisted in our final preparations. He proved to be a tremendously competent and affable man of about fifty, admirably well-read, and deeply familiar with all the conditions of Australian travel. He had tractors waiting at Pilbarra, and we chartered a tramp steamer of sufficiently light draught to get up the river to that point. We were prepared to excavate in the most careful and scientific fashion, sifting every particle of sand, and disturbing nothing which might seem to be in or near its original situation.

Sailing from Boston aboard the wheezy *Lexington* on March 28, 1935, we had a leisurely trip across the Atlantic and Mediterranean, through the Suez Canal, down the Red Sea, and across the Indian Ocean to our goal. I need not tell how the sight of the low, sandy West Australian coast depressed me, and how I detested the crude mining town and dreary gold fields where the tractors were given their last loads. Dr. Boyle, who met us, proved to be elderly, pleasant, and intelligent—and his knowledge of psychology led him into many long discussions with my son and me.

Discomfort and expectancy were oddly mingled in most of us when at length our party of eighteen rattled forth over the arid leagues of sand and rock. On Friday, May 31st, we forded a branch of the De Grey and entered the realm of utter desolation. A certain positive terror grew on me as we advanced to this actual site of the elder world behind the legends—a terror of course abetted by the fact that my disturbing dreams and pseudo-memories still beset me with unabated force.

It was on Monday, June 3, that we saw the first of the half-buried blocks. I cannot describe the emotions with which I actually touched—in objective reality—a fragment of Cyclopean masonry in every respect like the blocks in the walls of my dream-buildings. There was a distinct trace of carving—and my hands trembled as I recognised part of a curvilinear decorative scheme made hellish to me through years of tormenting nightmare and baffling research.

A month of digging brought a total of some 1250 blocks in varying stages of wear and disintegration. Most of these were carven megaliths with curved tops and bottoms. A minority were smaller, flatter, plain-surfaced, and square or octagonally cut—like those of the floors and pavements in my dreams—while a few were singularly massive and curved or slanted in such a manner as to suggest use in vaulting or groining, or as parts of arches or round window casings. The deeper—and the farther north and east—we dug, the more blocks we found; though we still failed to discover any trace of arrangement among them. Professor Dyer was appalled at the measureless age of the fragments, and Freeborn found traces of symbols which fitted darkly into certain Papuan and Polynesian legends of infinite antiquity. The condition and scattering of the blocks told mutely of vertiginous cycles of time and geologic upheavals of cosmic savagery.

We had an aëroplane with us, and my son Wingate would often go up to different heights and scan the sand-and-rock waste for signs of dim, large-scale outlines—either differences of level or trails of scattered blocks. His results were virtually negative; for whenever he would one day think he had glimpsed some significant trend, he would on his next trip find the impression replaced by another equally insubstantial—a result of the shifting, wind-blown sand. One or two of these ephemeral suggestions, though, affected me queerly and disagreeably. They seemed, after a fashion, to dovetail horribly with something which I had dreamed or read, but which I could no longer remember. There was a terrible *pseudo-familiarity* about them—which somehow made me look furtively and apprehensively over the abominable, sterile terrain toward the north and northeast.

Around the first week in July I developed an unaccountable set of mixed emotions about that general northeasterly region. There was horror, and there was curiosity—but more than that, there was a persistent and perplexing illusion of *memory*. I tried all sorts of psychological expedients to get these notions out of my head, but met with no success. Sleeplessness also gained upon me, but I almost welcomed this because of the resultant shortening of my dream-periods. I acquired the habit of taking long, lone walks in the desert late at night—usually to the north or northeast, whither the sum of my strange new impulses seemed subtly to pull me.

Sometimes, on these walks, I would stumble over nearly buried fragments of the ancient masonry. Though there were fewer visible blocks here than where we had started, I felt sure that there must be a vast abundance beneath the surface. The ground was less level than at our camp, and the prevailing high winds now and then piled the sand into fantastic temporary hillocks—exposing some traces of the elder stones while it covered other traces. I was queerly anxious to have the excavations extend to this territory, yet at the same time dreaded what might be revealed. Obviously, I was getting into a rather bad state—all the worse because I could not account for it.

An indication of my poor nervous health can be gained from my response to an odd discovery which I made on one of my nocturnal rambles. It was on the evening of July 11th, when a gibbous moon flooded the mysterious hillocks with a curious pallor. Wandering somewhat beyond my usual limits, I came upon a great stone which seemed to differ markedly from any we had yet encountered. It was almost wholly covered, but I stooped and cleared away the sand with my hands, later studying the object carefully and supplementing the moonlight with my electric torch. Unlike the other very large rocks, this one was perfectly square-cut, with no convex or concave surface. It seemed, too, to be of a dark basaltic substance wholly dissimilar to the granite and sandstone and occasional concrete of the now familiar fragments.

Suddenly I rose, turned, and ran for the camp at top speed. It was a wholly unconscious and irrational flight, and only when I was close to my tent did I fully realise why I had run. Then it came to me. The queer dark stone was something which I had dreamed and read about, and which was linked with the uttermost horrors of the aeon-old legendry. It was one of the blocks of that basaltic elder masonry which the fabled Great Race held in such fear—the tall, windowless ruins left by those brooding, half-material, alien Things that festered in earth's nether abysses and against whose wind-like, invisible forces the trap-doors were sealed and the sleepless sentinels posted.

I remained awake all that night, but by dawn realised how silly I had been to let the shadow of a myth upset me. Instead of being frightened, I should have had a discoverer's enthusiasm. The next forenoon I told the others about my find, and Dyer, Freeborn, Boyle, my son, and I set out to view the anomalous block. Failure, however, confronted us. I had formed no clear idea of the stone's location, and a late wind had wholly altered the hillocks of shifting sand.

VI

I come now to the crucial and most difficult part of my narrative—all the more difficult because I cannot be quite certain of its reality. At times I feel uncomfortably sure that I was not dreaming or deluded; and it is this feeling—in view of the stupendous implications which the objective truth of my experience would raise—which impels me to make this record. My son—a trained psychologist with the fullest and most sympathetic knowledge of my whole case—shall be the primary judge of what I have to tell.

First let me outline the externals of the matter, as those at the camp know them. On the night of July 17–18, after a windy day, I retired early but could not sleep. Rising shortly before eleven, and afflicted as usual with that strange feeling regarding the northeastward terrain, I set out on one of my typical nocturnal walks; seeing and greeting only one person—an Australian miner named Tupper—as I left our precincts. The moon, slightly past full, shone from a clear sky and drenched the ancient sands with a white, leprous radiance which seemed to me somehow infinitely evil. There was no longer any wind, nor did any return for nearly five hours, as amply attested by Tupper and others who did not sleep through the night. The Australian last saw me walking rapidly across the pallid, secret-guarding hillocks toward the northeast.

About 3:30 a.m. a violent wind blew up, waking everyone in camp and felling three of the tents. The sky was unclouded, and the desert still blazed with that leprous moonlight. As the party saw to the tents my absence was noted, but in view of my previous walks this circumstance gave no one alarm. And yet as many as three men—all Australians— seemed to feel something sinister in the air. Mackenzie explained to Prof. Freeborn that this was a fear picked up from blackfellow folk- lore—the natives having woven a curious fabric of malignant myth about the high winds which at long intervals sweep across the sands under a clear sky. Such winds, it is whispered, blow out of the great stone huts under the ground where terrible things have happened— and are never felt except near places where the big marked stones are scattered. Close to four the gale subsided as suddenly as it had begun, leaving the sand hills in new and unfamiliar shapes.

It was just past five, with the bloated, fungoid moon sinking in the west, when I staggered into camp—hatless, tattered, features scratched and ensanguined, and without my electric torch. Most of the men had returned to bed, but Prof. Dyer was smoking a pipe in front of his tent. Seeing my winded and almost frenzied state, he called Dr. Boyle, and the two of them got me on my cot and made me comfortable. My son, roused by the stir, soon joined them, and they all tried to force me to lie still and attempt sleep.

But there was no sleep for me. My psychological state was very extraordinary—different from anything I had previously suffered. After a time I insisted upon talking—nervously and elaborately explaining my condition. I told them I had become fatigued, and had lain down in the sand for a nap. There had, I said, been dreams even more frightful than usual—and when I was awaked by the sudden high wind my overwrought nerves had snapped. I had fled in panic, frequently falling over half-buried stones and thus gaining my tattered and bedraggled aspect. I must have slept long—hence the hours of my absence.

Of anything strange either seen or experienced I hinted absolutely nothing—exercising the greatest self-control in that respect. But I spoke of a change of mind regarding the whole work of the expedition, and earnestly urged a halt in all digging toward the northeast. My reasoning was patently weak—for I mentioned a dearth of blocks, a wish not to offend the superstitious miners, a possible shortage of funds from the college, and other things either untrue or irrelevant. Naturally, no one paid the least attention to my new wishes—not even my son, whose concern for my health was very obvious.

The next day I was up and around the camp, but took no part in the excavations. Seeing that I could not stop the work, I decided to return home as soon as possible for the sake of my nerves, and made my son promise to fly me in the plane to Perth—a thousand miles to the southwest—as soon as he had surveyed the region I wished let alone. If, I reflected, the thing I had seen was still visible, I might decide to attempt a specific warning even at the cost of ridicule. It was just conceivable that the miners who knew the local folklore might back me up. Humouring me, my son made the survey that very afternoon; flying over all the terrain my walk could possibly have covered. Yet nothing of what I had found remained in sight. It was the case of the anomalous basalt block all over again—the shifting sand had wiped out every trace. For an instant I half regretted having lost a certain awesome object in my stark fright—but now I know that the loss was merciful. I can still believe my whole experience an illusion—especially if, as I devoutly hope, that hellish abyss is never found.

Wingate took me to Perth July 20, though declining to abandon the expedition and return home. He stayed with me until the 25th, when the steamer for Liverpool sailed. Now, in the cabin of the *Empress*, I am pondering long and frantically on the entire matter, and have decided that my son at least must be informed. It shall rest with him whether to diffuse the matter more widely. In order to meet any eventuality I have prepared this summary of my background—as already known in a scattered way to others—and will now tell as briefly as possible what seemed to happen during my absence from the camp that hideous night.

Nerves on edge, and whipped into a kind of perverse eagerness by that inexplicable, dread-mingled, pseudo-mnemonic urge toward the northeast, I plodded on beneath the evil, burning moon. Here and there I saw, half-shrouded by the sand, those primal Cyclopean blocks left from nameless and forgotten aeons. The incalculable age and brooding horror of this monstrous waste began to oppress me as never before, and I could not keep from thinking of my maddening dreams, of the frightful legends which lay behind them, and of the present fears of natives and miners concerning the desert and its carven stones.

And yet I plodded on as if to some eldritch rendezvous—more and more assailed by bewildering fancies, compulsions, and pseudo-memories. I thought of some of the possible contours of the lines of stones as seen by my son from the air, and wondered why they seemed at once so ominous and so familiar. Something was fumbling and rattling at the latch of my recollection, while another unknown force sought to keep the portal barred.

The night was windless, and the pallid sand curved upward and downward like frozen waves of the sea. I had no goal, but somehow ploughed along as if with fate-bound assurance. My dreams welled up into the waking world, so that each sand-embedded megalith seemed part of endless rooms and corridors of pre-human masonry, carved and hieroglyphed with symbols that I knew too well from years of custom as a captive mind of the Great Race. At moments I fancied I saw those omniscient conical horrors moving about at their accustomed tasks, and I feared to look down lest I find myself one with them in aspect. Yet all the while I saw the sand-covered blocks as well as the rooms and corridors; the evil, burning moon as well as the lamps of luminous crystal; the endless desert as well as the waving ferns and cycads beyond the windows. I was awake and dreaming at the same time.

I do not know how long or how far—or indeed, in just what direction—I had walked when I first spied the heap of blocks bared by the

And yet I plodded on as if to some eldritch rendezvous . . .

. . . more and more assailed by bewildering fancies, compulsions, and pseudo-memories.

day's wind. It was the largest group in one place that I had so far seen, and so sharply did it impress me that the visions of fabulous aeons faded suddenly away. Again there were only the desert and the evil moon and the shards of an unguessed past. I drew close and paused, and cast the added light of my electric torch over the tumbled pile. A hillock had blown away, leaving a low, irregularly round mass of megaliths and smaller fragments some forty feet across and from two to eight feet high.

From the very outset I realised that there was some utterly unprecedented quality about these stones. Not only was the mere number of them quite without parallel, but something in the sand-worn traces of design arrested me as I scanned them under the mingled beams of the moon and my torch. Not that any one differed essentially from the earlier specimens we had found. It was something subtler than that. The impression did not come when I looked at one block alone, but only when I ran my eye over several almost simultaneously. Then, at last, the truth dawned upon me. The curvilinear patterns on many of these blocks were *closely related*—parts of one vast decorative conception. For the first time in this aeon-shaken waste I had come upon a mass of masonry in its old position—tumbled and fragmentary, it is true, but none the less existing in a very definite sense.

Mounting at a low place, I clambered laboriously over the heap; here and there clearing away the sand with my fingers, and constantly striving to interpret varieties of size, shape, and style, and relationships of design. After a while I could vaguely guess at the nature of the bygone structure, and at the designs which had once stretched over the vast surfaces of the primal masonry. The perfect identity of the whole with some of my dream-glimpses appalled and unnerved me. This was once a Cyclopean corridor thirty feet tall, paved with octagonal blocks and solidly vaulted overhead. There would have been rooms opening off on the right, and at the farther end one of those strange inclined planes would have wound down to still lower depths.

I started violently as these conceptions occurred to me, for there was more in them than the blocks themselves had supplied. How did I know that this level should have been far underground? How did I know that the plane leading upward should have been behind me? How did I know that the long subterrene passage to the Square of Pillars ought to lie on the left one level above me? How did I know that the room of machines, and the rightward-leading tunnel to the central archives, ought to lie two levels below? How did I know that there would be one of those horrible, metal-banded trap-doors at the very bottom, four levels down? Bewildered by this intrusion from the dream-world, I found myself shaking and bathed in a cold perspiration.

Then, as a last, intolerable touch, I felt that faint, insidious stream of cool air trickling upward from a depressed place near the centre of the huge heap. Instantly, as once before, my visions faded, and I saw again only the evil moonlight, the brooding desert, and the spreading tumulus of palaeogean masonry. Something real and tangible, yet fraught with infinite suggestions of nighted mystery, now confronted me. For that stream of air could argue but one thing—a hidden gulf of great size beneath the disordered blocks on the surface.

My first thought was of the sinister blackfellow legends of vast underground huts among the megaliths where horrors happen and great winds are born. Then thoughts of my own dreams came back, and I felt dim pseudo-memories tugging at my mind. What manner of place lay below me? What primal, inconceivable source of age-old myth-cycles and haunting nightmares might I be on the brink of uncovering? It was only for a moment that I hesitated, for more than curiosity and scientific zeal was driving me on and working against my growing fear.

I seemed to move almost automatically, as if in the clutch of some compelling fate. Pocketing my torch, and struggling with a strength that I had not thought I possessed, I wrenched aside first one titan fragment of stone and then another, till there welled up a strong draught whose dampness contrasted oddly with the desert's dry air. A black rift began to yawn, and at length—when I had pushed away every fragment small enough to budge—the leprous moonlight blazed on an aperture of ample width to admit me.

I drew out my torch and cast a brilliant beam into the opening. Below me was a chaos of tumbled masonry, sloping roughly down toward the north at an angle of about forty-five degrees, and evidently the result of some bygone collapse from above. Between its surface and the ground level was a gulf of impenetrable blackness at whose upper edge were signs of gigantic, stress-heaved vaulting. At this point, it appeared, the desert's sands lay directly upon a floor of some titan structure of earth's youth—how preserved through aeons of geologic convulsion I could not then and cannot now even attempt to guess.

In retrospect, the barest idea of a sudden, lone descent into such a doubtful abyss—and at a time when one's whereabouts were unknown to any living soul—seems like the utter apex of insanity. Perhaps it was—yet that night I embarked without hesitancy upon such a descent. Again there was manifest that lure and driving of fatality which had all along seemed to direct my course. With torch flashing intermittently to save the battery, I commenced a mad scramble down the sinister, Cyclopean incline below the opening—sometimes facing forward as I found good hand and foot holds, and at other times turning to face the heap of megaliths as I clung and fumbled more precariously. In two directions beside me, distant walls of carven, crumbling masonry loomed dimly under the direct beams of my torch. Ahead, however, was only unbroken blackness.

I kept no track of time during my downward scramble. So seething with baffling hints and images was my mind, that all objective matters seemed withdrawn into incalculable distances. Physical sensation was dead, and even fear remained as a wraith-like, inactive gargoyle leering impotently at me. Eventually I reached a level floor strown with fallen blocks, shapeless fragments of stone, and sand and detritus of every kind. On either side—perhaps thirty feet apart—rose massive walls culminating in huge groinings. That they were carved I could just discern, but the nature of the carvings was beyond my perception. What held me the most was the vaulting overhead. The beam from my torch could not reach the roof, but the lower parts of the monstrous arches stood out distinctly. And so perfect was their identity with what I had seen in countless dreams of the elder world, that I trembled actively for the first time.

Behind and high above, a faint luminous blur told of the distant moonlit world outside. Some vague shred of caution warned me that I should not let it out of my sight, lest I have no guide for my return. I now advanced toward the wall on my left, where the traces of carving were plainest. The littered floor was nearly as hard to traverse as the downward heap had been, but I managed to pick my difficult way. At one place I heaved aside some blocks and kicked away the detritus to see what the pavement was like, and shuddered at the utter, fateful familiarity of the great octagonal stones whose buckled surface still held roughly together.

Reaching a convenient distance from the wall, I cast the torchlight slowly and carefully over its worn remnants of carving. Some bygone influx of water seemed to have acted on the sandstone surface, while there were curious incrustations which I could not explain. In places the masonry was very loose and distorted, and I wondered how many aeons more this primal, hidden edifice could keep its remaining traces of form amidst earth's heavings.

But it was the carvings themselves that excited me most. Despite their time-crumbled state, they were relatively easy to trace at close range; and the complete, intimate familiarity of every detail almost stunned my imagination. That the major attributes of this hoary masonry should be familiar, was not beyond normal credibility. Powerfully impressing the weavers of certain myths, they had become embodied in a stream of cryptic lore which, somehow coming to my notice during the amnesic period, had evoked vivid images in my subconscious mind. But how could I explain the exact and minute fashion in which each line and spiral of these strange designs tallied with what I had dreamt for more than a score of years? What obscure, forgotten iconography could have reproduced each subtle shading and nuance which so persistently, exactly, and unvaryingly besieged my sleeping vision night after night?

For this was no chance or remote resemblance. Definitely and absolutely, the millennially ancient, aeon-hidden corridor in which

I stood was the original of something I knew in sleep as intimately as I knew my own house in Crane Street, Arkham. True, my dreams shewed the place in its undecayed prime; but the identity was no less real on that account. I was wholly and horribly oriented. The particular structure I was in was known to me. Known, too, was its place in that terrible elder city of dreams. That I could visit unerringly any point in that structure or in that city which had escaped the changes and devastations of uncounted ages, I realised with hideous and instinctive certainty. What in God's name could all this mean? How had I come to know what I knew? And what awful reality could lie behind those antique tales of the beings who had dwelt in this labyrinth of primordial stone?

Words can convey only fractionally the welter of dread and bewilderment which ate at my spirit. I knew this place. I knew what lay before me, and what had lain overhead before the myriad towering stories had fallen to dust and debris and the desert. No need now, I thought with a shudder, to keep that faint blur of moonlight in view. I was torn betwixt a longing to flee and a feverish mixture of burning curiosity and driving fatality. What had happened to this monstrous megalopolis of eld in the millions of years since the time of my dreams? Of the subterrene mazes which had underlain the city and linked all its titan towers, how much had still survived the writhings of earth's crust?

Had I come upon a whole buried world of unholy archaism? Could I still find the house of the writing-master, and the tower where S'gg'ha, a captive mind from the star-headed vegetable carnivores of Antarctica, had chiselled certain pictures on the blank spaces of the walls? Would the passage at the second level down, to the hall of the alien minds, be still unchoked and traversable? In that hall the captive mind of an incredible entity—a half-plastic denizen of the hollow interior of an unknown trans-Plutonian planet eighteen million years in the future—had kept a certain thing which it had modelled from clay.

I shut my eyes and put my hand to my head in a vain, pitiful effort to drive these insane dream-fragments from my consciousness.

Then, for the first time, I felt acutely the coolness, motion, and dampness of the surrounding air. Shuddering, I realised that a vast chain of aeon-dead black gulfs must indeed be yawning somewhere beyond and below me. I thought of the frightful chambers and corridors and inclines as I recalled them from my dreams. Would the way to the central archives still be open? Again that driving fatality tugged insistently at my brain as I recalled the awesome records that once lay cased in those rectangular vaults of rustless metal.

There, said the dreams and legends, had reposed the whole history, past and future, of the cosmic space-time continuum—written by captive minds from every orb and every age in the solar system. Madness, of course—but had I not now stumbled into a nighted world as mad as I? I thought of the locked metal shelves, and of the curious knob-twistings needed to open each one. My own came vividly into my consciousness. How often had I gone through that intricate routine of varied turns and pressures in the terrestrial vertebrate section on the lowest level! Every detail was fresh and familiar. If there were such a vault as I had dreamed of, I could open it in a moment. It was then that madness took me utterly. An instant later, and I was leaping and stumbling over the rocky debris toward the well-remembered incline to the depths below.

VII

From that point forward my impressions are scarcely to be relied on—indeed, I still possess a final, desperate hope that they all form parts of some daemoniac dream—or illusion born of delirium. A fever raged in my brain, and everything came to me through a kind of haze—sometimes only intermittently. The rays of my torch shot feebly into the engulfing blackness, bringing phantasmal flashes of hideously familiar walls and carvings, all blighted with the decay of ages. In one place a tremendous mass of vaulting had fallen, so that I had to clamber over a mighty mound of stones reaching almost to the ragged, grotesquely stalactited roof. It was all the ultimate apex of nightmare, made worse by the blasphemous tug of pseudo-memory. One thing only was unfamiliar, and that was my own size in relation to the monstrous masonry. I felt oppressed by a sense of unwonted smallness, as if the sight of these towering walls from a mere human body was something wholly new and abnormal. Again and again I looked nervously down at myself, vaguely disturbed by the human form I possessed.

Onward through the blackness of the abyss I leaped, plunged, and staggered—often falling and bruising myself, and once nearly shattering my torch. Every stone and corner of that daemoniac gulf was known to me, and at many points I stopped to cast beams of light through choked and crumbling yet familiar archways. Some rooms had totally collapsed; others were bare or debris-filled. In a few I saw masses of metal—some fairly intact, some broken, and some crushed or battered—which I recognised as the colossal pedestals or tables of my dreams. What they could in truth have been, I dared not guess.

I found the downward incline and began its descent—though after a time halted by a gaping, ragged chasm whose narrowest point could not be much less than four feet across. Here the stonework had fallen through, revealing incalculable inky depths beneath. I knew there were two more cellar levels in this titan edifice, and trembled with fresh panic as I recalled the metal-clamped trap-door on the lowest one. There could be no guards now—for what had lurked beneath had long since done its hideous work and sunk into its long decline. By the time of the post-human beetle race it would be quite dead. And yet, as I thought of the native legends, I trembled anew.

It cost me a terrible effort to vault that yawning chasm, since the littered floor prevented a running start—but madness drove me on. I chose a place close to the left-hand wall—where the rift was least wide and the landing-spot reasonably clear of dangerous debris— and after one frantic moment reached the other side in safety. At last gaining the lower level, I stumbled on past the archway of the room of machines, within which were fantastic ruins of metal half-buried beneath fallen vaulting. Everything was where I knew it would be, and I climbed confidently over the heaps which barred the entrance of a vast transverse corridor. This, I realised, would take me under the city to the central archives.

Endless ages seemed to unroll as I stumbled, leaped, and crawled along that debris-cluttered corridor. Now and then I could make out carvings on the age-stained walls—some familiar, others seemingly added since the period of my dreams. Since this was a subterrene house-connecting highway, there were no archways save when the route led through the lower levels of various buildings. At some of these intersections I turned aside long enough to look down well-remembered corridors and into well-remembered rooms. Twice only did I find any radical changes from what I had dreamed of—and in one of these cases I could trace the sealed-up outlines of the archway I remembered.

I shook violently, and felt a curious surge of retarding weakness, as I steered a hurried and reluctant course through the crypt of one of those great windowless ruined towers whose alien basalt masonry bespoke a whispered and horrible origin. This primal vault was round and fully two hundred feet across, with nothing carved upon the dark-hued stonework. The floor was here free from anything save dust and sand, and I could see the apertures leading upward and downward. There were no stairs or inclines—indeed, my dreams had pictured those elder towers as wholly untouched by the fabulous Great Race. Those who had built them had not needed stairs or inclines. In the dreams, the downward aperture had been tightly sealed and nervously guarded. Now it lay open—black and yawning, and giving forth a current of cool, damp air. Of what limitless caverns of eternal night might brood below, I would not permit myself to think.

Later, clawing my way along a badly heaped section of the corridor, I reached a place where the roof had wholly caved in. The debris rose like a mountain, and I climbed up over it, passing through a vast empty space where my torchlight could reveal neither walls nor vaulting. This, I reflected, must be the cellar of the house of the metal-purveyors, fronting on the third square not far from the archives. What had happened to it I could not conjecture.

I found the corridor again beyond the mountain of detritus and stones, but after a short distance encountered a wholly choked place where the fallen vaulting almost touched the perilously sagging ceiling. How I managed to wrench and tear aside enough blocks to afford a passage, and how I dared disturb the tightly packed fragments when the least shift of equilibrium might have brought down all the tons of superincumbent masonry to crush me to nothingness,

I do not know. It was sheer madness that impelled and guided me—if, indeed, my whole underground adventure was not—as I hope—a hellish delusion or phase of dreaming. But I did make—or dream that I made—a passage that I could squirm through. As I wriggled over the mound of debris—my torch, switched continuously on, thrust deeply within my mouth—I felt myself torn by the fantastic stalactites of the jagged floor above me.

I was now close to the great underground archival structure which seemed to form my goal. Sliding and clambering down the farther side of the barrier, and picking my way along the remaining stretch of corridor with hand-held, intermittently flashing torch, I came at last to a low, circular crypt with arches—still in a marvellous state of preservation—opening off on every side. The walls, or such parts of them as lay within reach of my torchlight, were densely hieroglyphed and chiselled with typical curvilinear symbols—some added since the period of my dreams.

This, I realised, was my fated destination, and I turned at once through a familiar archway on my left. That I could find a clear passage up and down the incline to all the surviving levels, I had oddly little doubt. This vast, earth-protected pile, housing the annals of all the solar system, had been built with supernal skill and strength to last as long as that system itself. Blocks of stupendous size, poised with mathematical genius and bound with cements of incredible toughness, had combined to form a mass as firm as the planet's rocky core. Here, after ages more prodigious than I could sanely grasp, its buried bulk stood in all its essential contours; the vast, dust-drifted floors scarce sprinkled with the litter elsewhere so dominant.

The relatively easy walking from this point onward went curiously to my head. All the frantic eagerness hitherto frustrated by obstacles now took itself out in a kind of febrile speed, and I literally raced along the low-roofed, monstrously well-remembered aisles beyond the archway. I was past being astonished by the familiarity of what I saw. On every hand the great hieroglyphed metal shelf-doors loomed monstrously; some yet in place, others sprung open, and still others bent and buckled under bygone geological stresses not quite strong enough to shatter the titan masonry. Here and there a dust-covered heap below a gaping empty shelf seemed to indicate where cases had been shaken down by earth-tremors. On occasional pillars were great symbols or letters proclaiming classes and sub-classes of volumes.

Once I paused before an open vault where I saw some of the accustomed metal cases still in position amidst the omnipresent gritty dust. Reaching up, I dislodged one of the thinner specimens with some difficulty, and rested it on the floor for inspection. It was titled in the prevailing curvilinear hieroglyphs, though something in the arrangement of the characters seemed subtly unusual. The odd mechanism of the hooked fastener was perfectly well known to me, and I snapped up the still rustless and workable lid and drew out the book within. The latter, as expected, was some twenty by fifteen inches in area, and two inches thick; the thin metal covers opening at the top. Its tough cellulose pages seemed unaffected by the myriad cycles of time they had lived through, and I studied the queerly pigmented, brush-drawn letters of the text—symbols utterly unlike either the usual curved hieroglyphs or any alphabet known to human scholarship—with a haunting, half-aroused memory. It came to me that this was the language used by a captive mind I had known slightly in my dreams—a mind from a large asteroid on which had survived much of the archaic life and lore of the primal planet whereof it formed a fragment. At the same time I recalled that this level of the archives was devoted to volumes dealing with the non-terrestrial planets.

As I ceased poring over this incredible document I saw that the light of my torch was beginning to fail, hence quickly inserted the extra battery I always had with me. Then, armed with the stronger radiance, I resumed my feverish racing through unending tangles of aisles and corridors—recognising now and then some familiar shelf, and vaguely annoyed by the acoustic conditions which made my footfalls echo incongruously in these catacombs of aeon-long death and silence. The very prints of my shoes behind me in the millennially untrodden dust made me shudder. Never before, if my mad dreams held anything of truth, had human feet pressed upon those immemorial pavements. Of the particular goal of my insane racing, my conscious mind held no hint. There was, however, some force of evil potency pulling at my dazed will and buried recollections, so that I vaguely felt I was not running at random.

I came to a downward incline and followed it to profounder depths. Floors flashed by me as I raced, but I did not pause to explore them. In my whirling brain there had begun to beat a certain rhythm which set my right hand twitching in unison. I wanted to unlock something, and felt that I knew all the intricate twists and pressures needed to do it. It would be like a modern safe with a combination lock. Dream or not, I had once known and still knew. How any dream—or scrap of unconsciously absorbed legend—could have taught me a detail so minute, so intricate, and so complex, I did not attempt to explain to myself. I was beyond all coherent thought. For was not this whole experience—this shocking familiarity with a set of unknown ruins, and this monstrously exact identity of everything before me with what only dreams and scraps of myth could have suggested—a horror beyond all reason? Probably it was my basic conviction then—as it is now during my saner moments—that I was not awake at all, and that the entire buried city was a fragment of febrile hallucination.

Eventually I reached the lowest level and struck off to the right of the incline. For some shadowy reason I tried to soften my steps, even though I lost speed thereby. There was a space I was afraid to cross on this last, deeply buried floor, and as I drew near it I recalled what thing in that space I feared. It was merely one of the metal-barred and closely guarded trap-doors. There would be no guards now, and on that account I trembled and tiptoed as I had done in passing through that black basalt vault where a similar trap-door had yawned. I felt a current of cool, damp air, as I had felt there, and wished that my course led in another direction. Why I had to take the particular course I was taking, I did not know.

When I came to the space I saw that the trap-door yawned widely open. Ahead the shelves began again, and I glimpsed on the floor before one of them a heap very thinly covered with dust, where a number of cases had recently fallen. At the same moment a fresh wave of panic clutched me, though for some time I could not discover why. Heaps of fallen cases were not uncommon, for all through the aeons this lightless labyrinth had been racked by the heavings of earth and had echoed at intervals to the deafening clatter of toppling objects. It was only when I was nearly across the space that I realised why I shook so violently.

Not the heap, but something about the dust of the level floor was troubling me. In the light of my torch it seemed as if that dust were not as even as it ought to be—there were places where it looked thinner, as if it had been disturbed not many months before. I could not be sure, for even the apparently thinner places were dusty enough; yet a certain suspicion of regularity in the fancied unevenness was highly disquieting. When I brought the torchlight close to one of the queer places I did not like what I saw—for the illusion of regularity became very great. It was as if there were regular lines of composite impressions—impressions that went in threes, each slightly over a foot square, and consisting of five nearly circular three-inch prints, one in advance of the other four.

These possible lines of foot-square impressions appeared to lead in two directions, as if something had gone somewhere and returned. They were of course very faint, and may have been illusions or accidents; but there was an element of dim, fumbling terror about the way I thought they ran. For at one end of them was the heap of cases which must have clattered down not long before, while at the other end was the ominous trap-door with the cool, damp wind, yawning unguarded down to abysses past imagination.

VIII

That my strange sense of compulsion was deep and overwhelming is shewn by its conquest of my fear. No rational motive could have drawn me on after that hideous suspicion of prints and the creeping dream-memories it excited. Yet my right hand, even as it shook with fright, still twitched rhythmically in its eagerness to turn a lock it hoped to find. Before I knew it I was past the heap of lately fallen cases and running on tiptoe through aisles of utterly unbroken dust toward a point which I seemed to know morbidly, horribly well. My mind was asking itself questions whose origin and relevancy I was only beginning to guess. Would the shelf be reachable by a human body? Could my human hand master all the aeon-remembered motions of the lock? Would the lock be undamaged and workable? And what would I do—what dare I do—with what (as I now commenced to realise) I both hoped and feared to find? Would it prove the awesome, brain-shattering truth of something past normal conception, or shew only that I was dreaming?

The next I knew I had ceased my tiptoe racing and was standing still, staring at a row of maddeningly familiar hieroglyphed shelves. They were in a state of almost perfect preservation, and only three of the doors in this vicinity had sprung open. My feelings toward these shelves cannot be described—so utter and insistent was the sense of old acquaintance. I was looking high up, at a row near the top and wholly out of my reach, and wondering how I could climb to best advantage. An open door four rows from the bottom would help, and the locks of the closed doors formed possible holds for hands and feet. I would grip the torch between my teeth as I had in other places where both hands were needed. Above all, I must make no noise. How to get down what I wished to remove would be difficult, but I could probably hook its movable fastener in my coat collar and carry it like a knapsack. Again I wondered whether the lock would be undamaged. That I could repeat each familiar motion I had not the least doubt. But I hoped the thing would not scrape or creak—and that my hand could work it properly.

Even as I thought these things I had taken the torch in my mouth and begun to climb. The projecting locks were poor supports; but as I had expected, the opened shelf helped greatly. I used both the difficultly swinging door and the edge of the aperture itself in my ascent, and managed to avoid any loud creaking. Balanced on the upper edge of the door, and leaning far to my right, I could just reach the lock I sought. My fingers, half-numb from climbing, were very clumsy at first; but I soon saw that they were anatomically adequate. And the memory-rhythm was strong in them. Out of unknown gulfs of time the intricate secret motions had somehow reached my brain correctly in every detail—for after less than five minutes of trying there came a click whose familiarity was all the more startling because I had not consciously anticipated it. In another instant the metal door was slowly swinging open with only the faintest grating sound.

Dazedly I looked over the row of greyish case-ends thus exposed, and felt a tremendous surge of some wholly inexplicable emotion. Just within reach of my right hand was a case whose curving hieroglyphs made me shake with a pang infinitely more complex than one of mere fright. Still shaking, I managed to dislodge it amidst a shower of gritty flakes, and ease it over toward myself without any violent noise. Like the other case I had handled, it was slightly more than twenty by fifteen inches in size, with curved mathematical designs in low relief. In thickness it just exceeded three inches. Crudely wedging it between myself and the surface I was climbing, I fumbled with the fastener and finally got the hook free. Lifting the cover, I shifted the heavy object to my back, and let the hook catch hold of my collar. Hands now free, I awkwardly clambered down to the dusty floor, and prepared to inspect my prize.

Kneeling in the gritty dust, I swung the case around and rested it in front of me. My hands shook, and I dreaded to draw out the book within almost as much as I longed—and felt compelled—to do so. It had very gradually become clear to me what I ought to find, and this realisation nearly paralysed my faculties. If the thing were there—and if I were not dreaming—the implications would be quite beyond the power of the human spirit to bear. What tormented me most was my momentary inability to feel that my surroundings were a dream. The sense of reality was hideous—and again becomes so as I recall the scene.

At length I tremblingly pulled the book from its container and stared fascinatedly at the well-known hieroglyphs on the cover. It seemed to be in prime condition, and the curvilinear letters of the title held me in almost as hypnotised a state as if I could read them. Indeed, I cannot swear that I did not actually read them in some transient and terrible access of abnormal memory. I do not know how long it was before I dared to lift that thin metal cover. I temporised and made excuses to myself. I took the torch from my mouth and shut it off to save the battery. Then, in the dark, I screwed up my courage—finally lifting the cover without turning on the light. Last of all I did indeed flash the torch upon the exposed page—steeling myself in advance to suppress any sound no matter what I should find.

I looked for an instant, then almost collapsed. Clenching my teeth, however, I kept silence. I sank wholly to the floor and put a hand to my forehead amidst the engulfing blackness. What I dreaded and expected was there. Either I was dreaming, or time and space had become a mockery. I must be dreaming—but I would test the horror by carrying this thing back and shewing it to my son if it were indeed a reality. My head swam frightfully, even though there were no visible objects in the unbroken gloom to swirl around me. Ideas and images of the starkest terror—excited by vistas which my glimpse had opened up—began to throng in upon me and cloud my senses.

I thought of those possible prints in the dust, and trembled at the sound of my own breathing as I did so. Once again I flashed on the light and looked at the page as a serpent's victim may look at his destroyer's eyes and fangs. Then, with clumsy fingers in the dark, I closed the book, put it in its container, and snapped the lid and the curious hooked fastener. This was what I must carry back to the outer world if it truly existed—if the whole abyss truly existed—if I, and the world itself, truly existed.

Just when I tottered to my feet and commenced my return I cannot be certain. It comes to me oddly—as a measure of my sense of separation from the normal world—that I did not even once look at my watch during those hideous hours underground. Torch in hand, and with the ominous case under one arm, I eventually found myself tiptoeing in a kind of silent panic past the draught-giving abyss and those lurking suggestions of prints. I lessened my precautions as I climbed up the endless inclines, but could not shake off a shadow of apprehension which I had not felt on the downward journey.

I dreaded having to re-pass through that black basalt crypt that was older than the city itself, where cold draughts welled up from unguarded depths. I thought of that which the Great Race had feared, and of what might still be lurking—be it ever so weak and dying—down there. I thought of those possible five-circle prints and of what my dreams had told me of such prints—and of strange winds and whistling noises associated with them. And I thought of the tales of the modern blacks, wherein the horror of great winds and nameless subterrene ruins was dwelt upon.

I knew from a carven wall symbol the right floor to enter, and came at last—after passing that other book I had examined—to the great circular space with the branching archways. On my right, and at once recognisable, was the arch through which I had arrived. This I now entered, conscious that the rest of my course would be harder because of the tumbled state of the masonry outside the archive building. My new metal-cased burden weighed upon me, and I found it harder and harder to be quiet as I stumbled among debris and fragments of every sort.

Then I came to the ceiling-high mound of debris through which I had wrenched a scanty passage. My dread at wriggling through again was infinite; for my first passage had made some noise, and I now—after seeing those possible prints—dreaded sound above all things. The case, too, doubled the problem of traversing the narrow crevice. But I clambered up the barrier as best I could, and pushed the case through the aperture ahead of me. Then, torch in mouth, I scrambled through myself—my back torn as before by stalactites. As I tried to grasp the case again, it fell some distance ahead of me down the slope of the debris, making a disturbing clatter and arousing echoes which sent me into a cold perspiration. I lunged for it at once, and regained it without further noise—but a moment afterward the slipping of blocks under my feet raised a sudden and unprecedented din.

The din was my undoing. For, falsely or not, I thought I heard it answered in a terrible way from spaces far behind me. I thought I heard a shrill, whistling sound, like nothing else on earth, and beyond any adequate verbal description. It may have been only my imagination. If so, what followed has a grim irony—since, save for the panic of this thing, the second thing might never have happened.

As it was, my frenzy was absolute and unrelieved. Taking my torch in my hand and clutching feebly at the case, I leaped and bounded wildly ahead with no idea in my brain beyond a mad desire to race out of these nightmare ruins to the waking world of desert and moonlight which lay so far above. I hardly knew it when I reached the mountain of debris which towered into the vast blackness beyond the caved-in roof, and bruised and cut myself repeatedly in scrambling up its steep slope of jagged blocks and fragments. Then came the great disaster. Just as I blindly crossed the summit, unprepared for the sudden dip ahead, my feet slipped utterly and I found myself involved in a mangling avalanche of sliding masonry whose cannon-loud uproar split the black cavern air in a deafening series of earth-shaking reverberations.

I have no recollection of emerging from this chaos, but a momentary fragment of consciousness shews me as plunging and tripping and scrambling along the corridor amidst the clangour—case and torch still with me. Then, just as I approached that primal basalt crypt I had so dreaded, utter madness came. For as the echoes of the avalanche died down, there became audible a repetition of that frightful, alien whistling I thought I had heard before. This time there was no doubt about it—and what was worse, it came from a point not behind but *ahead of me.*

Probably I shrieked aloud then. I have a dim picture of myself as flying through the hellish basalt vault of the Elder Things, and hearing that damnable alien sound piping up from the open, unguarded door of limitless nether blacknesses. There was a wind, too—not merely a cool, damp draught, but a violent, purposeful blast belching savagely and frigidly from that abominable gulf whence the obscene whistling came.

There are memories of leaping and lurching over obstacles of every sort, with that torrent of wind and shrieking sound growing moment by moment, and seeming to curl and twist purposefully around me as it struck out wickedly from the spaces behind and beneath. Though in my rear, that wind had the odd effect of hindering instead of aiding my progress; as if it acted like a noose or lasso thrown around me. Heedless of the noise I made, I clattered over a great barrier of blocks and was again in the structure that led to the surface. I recall glimpsing the archway to the room of machines and almost crying out as I saw the incline leading down to where one of those blasphemous trap-doors must be yawning two levels below. But instead of crying out I muttered over and over to myself that this was all a dream from which I must soon awake. Perhaps I was in camp—

There are memories of leaping and lurching over obstacles of every sort . . .

perhaps I was at home in Arkham. As these hopes bolstered up my sanity I began to mount the incline to the higher level.

I knew, of course, that I had the four-foot cleft to re-cross, yet was too racked by other fears to realise the full horror until I came almost upon it. On my descent, the leap across had been easy—but could I clear the gap as readily when going uphill, and hampered by fright, exhaustion, the weight of the metal case, and the anomalous backward tug of that daemon wind? I thought of these things at the last moment, and thought also of the nameless entities which might be lurking in the black abysses below the chasm.

My wavering torch was growing feeble, but I could tell by some obscure memory when I neared the cleft. The chill blasts of wind and the nauseous whistling shrieks behind me were for the moment like a merciful opiate, dulling my imagination to the horror of the yawning gulf ahead. And then I became aware of the added blasts and whistling *in front of me*—tides of abomination surging up through the cleft itself from depths unimagined and unimaginable.

Now, indeed, the essence of pure nightmare was upon me. Sanity departed—and ignoring everything except the animal impulse of flight, I merely struggled and plunged upward over the incline's debris as if no gulf had existed. Then I saw the chasm's edge, leaped frenziedly with every ounce of strength I possessed, and was instantly engulfed in a pandaemoniac vortex of loathsome sound and utter, materially tangible blackness.

This is the end of my experience, so far as I can recall. Any further impressions belong wholly to the domain of phantasmagoric delirium. Dream, madness, and memory merged wildly together in a series of fantastic, fragmentary delusions which can have no relation to anything real. There was a hideous fall through incalculable leagues of viscous, sentient darkness, and a babel of noises utterly alien to all that we know of the earth and its organic life. Dormant, rudimentary senses seemed to start into vitality within me, telling of pits and voids peopled by floating horrors and leading to sunless crags and oceans and teeming cities of windowless basalt towers upon which no light ever shone.

Secrets of the primal planet and its immemorial aeons flashed through my brain without the aid of sight or sound, and there were known to me things which not even the wildest of my former dreams had ever suggested. And all the while cold fingers of damp vapour clutched and picked at me, and that eldritch, damnable whistling shrieked fiendishly above all the alternations of babel and silence in the whirlpools of darkness around.

Afterward there were visions of the Cyclopean city of my dreams— not in ruins, but just as I had dreamed of it. I was in my conical, non-human body again, and mingled with crowds of the Great Race and the captive minds who carried books up and down the lofty corridors and vast inclines. Then, superimposed upon these pictures, were frightful momentary flashes of a non-visual consciousness involving desperate struggles, a writhing free from clutching tentacles of whistling wind, an insane, bat-like flight through half-solid air, a feverish burrowing through the cyclone-whipped dark, and a wild stumbling and scrambling over fallen masonry.

Once there was a curious, intrusive flash of half-sight—a faint, diffuse suspicion of bluish radiance far overhead. Then there came a dream of wind-pursued climbing and crawling—of wriggling into a blaze of sardonic moonlight through a jumble of debris which slid and collapsed after me amidst a morbid hurricane. It was the evil, monotonous beating of that maddening moonlight which at last told me of the return of what I had once known as the objective, waking world.

I was clawing prone through the sands of the Australian desert, and around me shrieked such a tumult of wind as I had never before known on our planet's surface. My clothing was in rags, and my whole body was a mass of bruises and scratches. Full consciousness returned very slowly, and at no time could I tell just where true memory left off and delirious dream began. There had seemed to be a mound of titan blocks, an abyss beneath it, a monstrous revelation from the past, and a nightmare horror at the end—but how much of this was real? My flashlight was gone, and likewise any metal case I may have discovered. Had there been such a case—or any abyss—or any mound? Raising my head, I looked behind me, and saw only the sterile, undulant sands of the waste.

The daemon wind died down, and the bloated, fungoid moon sank reddeningly in the west. I lurched to my feet and began to stagger southwestward toward the camp. What in truth had happened to me? Had I merely collapsed in the desert and dragged a dream-racked body over miles of sand and buried blocks? If not, how could I bear to live any longer? For in this new doubt all my faith in the myth-born unreality of my visions dissolved once more into the hellish older doubting. If that abyss was real, then the Great Race was real—and its blasphemous reachings and seizures in the cosmos-wide vortex of time were no myths or nightmares, but a terrible, soul-shattering actuality.

Had I, in full hideous fact, been drawn back to a pre-human world of a hundred and fifty million years ago in those dark, baffling days of the amnesia? Had my present body been the vehicle of a frightful alien consciousness from palaeogean gulfs of time? Had I, as the captive mind of those shambling horrors, indeed known that accursed city of stone in its primordial heyday, and wriggled down those familiar corridors in the loathsome shape of my captor? Were those tormenting dreams of more than twenty years the offspring of stark, monstrous *memories*? Had I once veritably talked with minds from reachless corners of time and space, learned the universe's secrets past and to come, and written the annals of my own world for the metal cases of those titan archives? And were those others—those shocking Elder Things of the mad winds and daemon pipings—in truth a lingering, lurking menace, waiting and slowly weakening in black abysses while varied shapes of life drag out their multimillennial courses on the planet's age-racked surface?

I do not know. If that abyss and what it held were real, there is no hope. Then, all too truly, there lies upon this world of man a mocking and incredible shadow out of time. But mercifully, there is no proof that these things are other than fresh phases of my myth-born dreams. I did not bring back the metal case that would have been a proof, and so far those subterrene corridors have not been found. If the laws of the universe are kind, they will never be found. But I must tell my son what I saw or thought I saw, and let him use his judgment as a psychologist in gauging the reality of my experience, and communicating this account to others.

I have said that the awful truth behind my tortured years of dreaming hinges absolutely upon the actuality of what I thought I saw in those Cyclopean buried ruins. It has been hard for me literally to set down the crucial revelation, though no reader can have failed to guess it. Of course it lay in that book within the metal case—the case which I pried out of its forgotten lair amidst the undisturbed dust of a million centuries. No eye had seen, no hand had touched that book since the advent of man to this planet. And yet, when I flashed my torch upon it in that frightful megalithic abyss, I saw that the queerly pigmented letters on the brittle, aeon-browned cellulose pages were not indeed any nameless hieroglyphs of earth's youth. They were, instead, the letters of our familiar alphabet, spelling out the words of the English language in my own handwriting.

They were . . . spelling out the words of the English language in my own handwriting.

The Vanity of Existence
in "The Shadow out of Time"
by Paul Montelone

S chopenhauer grandly opens the second volume of his main work and masterpiece, *The World as Will and Representation*, with the following words:

> In endless space countless luminous spheres, round each of which some dozen smaller illuminated ones revolve, hot at the core and covered over with a hard cold crust; on this crust a mouldy film has produced living and knowing beings; this is empirical truth, the real, the world. Yet for a being who thinks it is a precarious position to stand on one of those numberless spheres freely floating in boundless space, without knowing whence or whither, and to be only one of innumerable similar beings that throng, press, and toil, restlessly and rapidly arising and passing away in beginning-less and endless time. (3)

This, one of three vigorous philosophical assaults which Schopenhauer brought against "human megalomania," is his "cosmological affront" (as aptly termed by Rudiger Safranski [3]); it is joined by a "biological affront" ("man is an animal, whose intelligence must compensate for a lack of instinct and for inadequate adaption to the living world") and a "psychological affront" ("our conscious ego is not master in its own house"); and its insight forms the basis of Schopenhauer's various but unswervingly pessimistic reflections on what he called *der Nichtigkeit des Daseyns,* or "the vanity of existence." I would like in this essay to consider Lovecraft's cosmic indifferentism in terms of this idea, specifically as it is expressed in his most melancholy and yet paradoxically his coldest work, "The Shadow out of Time." To assist in this task, I will divide the essay into three sections. In the first section, I will establish the nature of reality in the novella; in the second, I will show how existence is pictured as vain; and in the third, I will explore the implications that follow from the first two with respect to the sense or nonsense of life.

I. Always Being, Never Becoming

What is the nature of reality in "The Shadow out of Time"? Always being, never becoming. How was this inferred? As follows.

As readers know, certain members of the Great Race have the ability to exchange minds with any intellectually evolved life form of any era. They have the power "to project themselves into the past and future, even through gulfs of millions of years" in order to "study the lore of every age." The question may therefore be asked: what kind of reality would permit this? A partial answer is supplied by Peaslee, who notes in one place that "there [is] no such thing as time in its humanly accepted sense," and more specifically in another that "Dr. Albert Einstein . . . was rapidly reducing time to the status of a mere dimension." On the assumption of the fact of the Great Race's conquest of time, we may draw two conclusions from these statements: first, that humankind has misconceived the nature of time; and second, that in consequence it has misunderstood the nature of reality. Time is not, as we have supposed, a mere consecutiveness in space, and reality is not the mere content of an empirical present (a present, that is, whose 'stuff' is perpetually lost in an irretrievable past). Time is "a mere dimension," which means that it is reducible to space. Or to put it more precisely: temporal eventuality is fundamentally *coexistent*; in other words, seemingly consecutive events do not follow one another in time, but exist in space *side by side and all at once*. That is why Peaslee, after his apparent amnesia, has difficulty distinguishing "between consecutiveness and simultaneousness." As a human being, he instinctively comprehends events in (temporal) succession, but during the transfer he vaguely touches their (spatial) concurrence—and that in fact is how they are.

The picture of reality that results from these inferences could be described as follows. Everything that has ever happened, happens, or will happen, happens *Now*, that is to say, in a *transcendental present*, which (hypothetically conceived) would comprehend the cosmos as a whole, in both space and time. Reality could thus be likened to a long, printed text, which, laid out page by page under the lamp of the transcendental present, would contain every actual (but not possible) event. How this narrative is read would be how reality is experienced. Members of the Great Race, then, would be able to read, through the medium of mind-exchange, whatever section of it that they desired in whatever order; while races of inferior intellectual power (such as humankind) would be able to decipher only assigned and isolated portions of it, and that only in a particular way, reading from left to right, so to speak, from future to past, through the infinitesimally narrow prism of the empirical present.

Perhaps a second analogy would be more to the point.

Reality (as represented in the narrative) could be likened to an immutable, benighted landscape, whose every contour is every actual event. Focused illumination of its features would constitute empirical experience. Members of the Great Race, then, could be imagined as traversing freely over the surface of this terrain, lighting whatever portion of it that they wished to experience; while intellectually inferior races, such as humankind, would be able to light only the ground that immediately presented itself to them, and that only while moving (always moving) in one and only one direction, that is, from future to past. The totality of such illuminations would be the totality of sentient experience; and thus, to extend the analogy further, if a sun were to rise over this landscape and were to hang motionless at the meridian, producing a shadowless noon, that sun would be the transcendental present: it would reveal not only every actual event, but also how all events are, namely, side by side and all at once.

We should not make the mistake, however, of thinking that the dauntless light of a transcendental present can be approximated by the near-omniscience of the Great Race. Though it throws its beam widely, the Great Race is limited in both its mode and scope of empirical knowledge. Firstly, it is only through "the power of its keener minds" that it is able to transfer consciousness from one era to another. Secondly, it still must overleap, quite literally, temporal distance, "gulfs of millions of years" and the "chasm of time" generally (two metaphors which, incidentally, sanction my terrain analogy). Thirdly, it has limited access to knowledge of the past, which is "harder to glean than knowledge of the future." And finally and most importantly, the Great Race is still subject to a sort of vestigial temporality of consecutiveness: it is pursued by extinction, which overtakes its home planet, and which in the shape (or shapelessness) of the subterranean horrors will eventually consume its civilization on earth: "the race would again face death, yet would live through another forward migration of its best minds into the bodies of others who had a longer physical span ahead of them." So the Great Race never fully seizes the reality that abides in the transcendental present. Like every other knowing species, it is bound to the line of Becoming, and thus, like them, it forever approaches but never reaches the asymptote of Being. Being is comprehended by the transcendental present, and in that present, which I am asserting only hypothetically on the basis of the time-traveling capability of the Great Race, there would be no passing away, no becoming, and all existence (though not all possibilities of existence) would stand forever. Every event, every contour on the terrain of eventuality, would ceaselessly exhibit itself: they would always be, and would never become.

II. Always Becoming, Never Being

The ultimate inaccessibility of Being condemns all knowing life-forms to eternal Becoming. Deprived of full and certain knowledge of the absolute nature of reality, they persist in an elusive shadow-world which is the product of their imperfect understanding. In "The Shadow out of Time" this condition is demonstrated by Peaslee, who is subjected to an experience that is at once laughably absurd and cruelly random, at least from his perspective (one among many in the Becoming), and who ultimately lays out for the contemplation of the reader a metaphysically horrific cosmos. In this section I will explore in detail these three aspects of Peaslee's experience.

Peaslee's experience is so absurd that I'm almost inclined to agree with Edmund Wilson when he implied with the title of his notorious Lovecraft essay ("Tales of the Marvellous and Ridiculous") that Lovecraft's novella is ridiculous. But my inclination stems not from the tale's failure (in which Wilson believes) but from its success. Peaslee's experience is ridiculous. Here is a protagonist, let us recall, a staid, unassuming, unimaginative, dedicated professor of Political Economy, who, without warning, is metamorphosed into a gargantuan, cone-shaped, note-taking alien vegetable. And here also is said vegetable who, in search of fresh knowledge and experience, is metamorphosed into a diminutive, rod-shaped, lecture-giving academic mammal. If comedy is grounded in a felicitous incongruities, then this is comic. And it surely is, especially when we later read of Peaslee's discovery of the change, revealed to him in a dream, which instigated a bout of screaming that "waked half of Arkham"—a nice hyperbole that may be adequately appreciated with a little imagination in regard to Peaslee's bewildered neighbors. But even more nearly hilarious is the truly *outré* jack-in-the-box image which inspires the hapless professor's nocturnal hysterics: "And then the morbid temptation to look down at myself became greater and greater, till one night I could not resist it.

At first my downward glance revealed nothing whatever. A moment later I perceived that this was because my head lay at the end of a flexible neck of enormous length." What is this, I ask, but a sight gag? And what, then, is the entire episode but a sort of extraterrestrial slapstick, with Peaslee pratfalling into Maurice Lévy's (68) abysm of time?

But the hilarity that underlies this episode is belied by the serious tone of Peaslee's exposition. One could laugh, but one does not (as Arthur Jean Cox [59] has pointed out about many Lovecraftian episodes generally). The whole thing is actually reminiscent of a more famous literary metamorphosis, that of Kafka's Gregor Samsa. Like Peaslee's change, Samsa's is discovered in bed: "As Gregor Samsa awoke one morning from uneasy dreams he found himself transformed in his bed into a gigantic insect" (67). Samsa's legs "waved helpless before his eyes" (67) just as Peaslee's 'head' vacillated hideously at the summit of a prodigious neck. Kafka, of course, was not writing for laughs, and neither was Lovecraft; but grotesque transformations are certainly sources of pathetic comedy. At the denouement, for instance, of the singularly dismal Laurel and Hardy short subject, *Below Zero*, a beaten and unconscious Stan awakes in and then emerges from a barrel that moments earlier was filled to the brim with frigid water: poor Stan is bloated nearly to the bursting point. That this remarkable film[1] wavers uncertainly between delight and despair suggests as well as any other artistic work how proximate the laughable and the pitiable are to one another. Lovecraft himself observed:

The wise to care a comic strain apply,
And shake with laughter, that they may not cry.
(*Miscellaneous Writings* 157)

So when one reads how the Yithian inhabiting Peaslee's cranium repeatedly (and idiotically) lets slip certain bits of anachronistic information about the course of terrestrial history, one does not

---

1 The comparison of Laurel and Hardy with Lovecraft and Kafka is not quite arbitrary, as corporeal metamorphosis is a recurrent motif in the former's work.

quite laugh but, rather, amusedly wonders over the acclaimed near-omniscience of a 'Great' Race which, in spite of its reputation and archives, seems to get bogged down by details: "I would inadvertently refer, with casual assurance, to specific events in dim ages outside the range of accepted history—passing off such references as a jest when I saw the surprise they created. And I had a way of speaking of the future which two or three times caused actual fright." These are really amazing blunders and are scarcely as excusable as the entity's imperfect grasp of language and custom. Still, they are not nearly as ridiculous as the reactions displayed by the thing's interlocutors. Are these people insightful or stupid? On the one hand, they seem to have unconsciously intuited the "outside" character of the Peaslee-usurper, and thus, like the dogs in "The Dunwich Horror" may have instinctively grasped the situation without having the wits to really understand it. And on the other hand, they display an astounding credulity over the allegedly prophetic utterances of an individual whom they regard as mentally unbalanced. But in either case, they are demeaned; and in the final analysis, so is the Great Race, which, despite the fact that it pulls off the transfer, just manages to cover its shortcomings with a "carefully veiled mockery."

The human race, however, bears the brunt of the absurd, which means that pea-like Peaslee gets it the most. Peaslee's experience initially presents itself as inexplicable and undeserved. On Thursday, May 14, 1908, at about 10:20 A.M. Peaslee collapses. He is in the middle of a class on Political Economy, lecturing to students, "juniors and a few sophomores," when, after some mental disturbance, he falls unconscious. In describing this event Peaslee is careful to point out that it has no precedent in his own life or in those of his forebears: "my own ancestry and background are altogether normal," he asserts; "there is nothing whatever of the mad or sinister in my heredity and early life." These statements, separated as they are by little other matter, are very nearly redundant and thus Peaslee, while not quite making himself hoarse, certainly wants to convey in the strongest possible terms the unanticipated nature of the event. "The thing" was indeed "quite sudden."

A comparison with Kafka's "The Metamorphosis" is again appropriate.[2] Like Peaslee's change, Samsa's is without personal or familial precedent. He merely wakes up one morning to find that he has become a giant cockroach. And like a hapless victim of the Yithian mind-exchange, he becomes "reconciled" to his repulsive shape. Confined to his bedroom, clinging to its walls, and eating the rubbish that his sister brings, Samsa carries on. But eventually his family rejects him: "We must try to get rid of it," his sister exclaims to her parents, no longer thinking of the insect as her brother; "If this were Gregor, he would have realized long ago that human beings can't live with such a creature, and he'd have gone away on his own accord" (125). Peaslee, evidently, receives similar treatment. "For thirteen years my life ran smoothly and happily," he says, dating his happiness from the beginning of his academic career and including within its scope such festive events as his marriage and the births of his three children; but after his change, Peaslee loses almost everything:

From the moment of my strange waking my wife had regarded me with extreme horror and loathing, vowing that I was some utter alien usurping the body of her husband. In 1910 she obtained a legal divorce, nor would she ever consent to see me, even after my return to normality in 1913. These feeling were shared by my elder son and my small daughter, neither of whom I have ever seen since.

This statement so understates Peaslee's suffering that it well-nigh highlights itself. And if we accept Kenneth W. Faig, Jr.'s (56–57) hypothesis that Peaslee has a prototype in Winfield Scott Lovecraft, Lovecraft's father, it would hardly be farfetched to assume that the passage is obliquely informed by Lovecraft's personal pain. In fact, it becomes a virtual certainty when we consider S. T. Joshi's observation that "Peaslee's amnesia dates from 1908 to 1913, the exact time when Lovecraft himself, having had to withdraw from high school,

---

[2] We may incidentally note here that Kafka and Lovecraft possess common philosophical ancestry in Schopenhauer.

descended into hermitry" (27). Certainly Peaslee wants to make sense of his persistent dreams, but in addition to this he undoubtedly wants an explanation for the unasked and undeserved disruption of the course of his life, a life which up until the collapse went, as he explicitly says, "smoothly and happily." The problem is that in attempting to make sense of his own life, Peaslee merely pushes the dilemma of meaning back. The more sense he makes of those few anomalous years of forgetfulness, the more senseless becomes his existence generally, until, at last and irrevocably, it engulfs all human existence.

But human existence is not only meaningless: as a form of life, it is also terrible. This fundamental proposition of pessimism, which is succinctly expressed in the Lovecraftian dictum that "[l]ife is more horrible than death" (*Miscellaneous Writings* 89), leads us to our final observation in this section, namely that Peaslee's dreams, though seemingly a mere stairwell to the ruins of human significance, are just as emphatically a symbolizing end in themselves.

As Peaslee's dreams gradually resolve themselves from vague non-visual feelings concerning "more abstract matters" into increasingly distinct and vivid memories, his horror mounts. But because Peaslee stands for all humanity, his horror cannot be regarded as either personal or idiosyncratic. His reaction expresses, rather, a kind of objective understanding. But an understanding of what? In fact, of life: as given, Peaslee's dreams trace in imagistic form *the inexorable production and evolution of life*.

Peaslee's first clear recollections are of various material things and structures. He sees an "enormous vaulted chamber," "colossal, round windows," "high, arched doors," "pedestals or tables," "[v]ast shelves," books "of immense size," "dark granite masonry," "papers," "writing materials," "lamps," "inexplicable machines," a "floor . . . of massive octagonal flagstones," and "Cyclopean corridors of stone." He also views from the window and from a "titanic flat roof," (whose area is "wide" and "barren" and which features a "scalloped parapet of stone") "endless leagues of giant buildings," "paved roads" and "enormous dark cylindrical towers." The point here is that nearly every object that Peaslee first recalls is *insentient*, and yet, they are also as such to imply the presence of life. That is to say, they ensure life because a living someone or something has obviously made them. Accordingly, they may be likened to mere matter, which in itself does not live, but which by its very nature necessitates life (I presume here a Lovecraftian determinism, not a naive theism). The imagery, then, partially discloses the pessimistic basis of Peaslee's vague feeling of foreboding. This emerges more sharply as his memories clarify.

Life is introduced gradually, first glimpsed as vegetation—"the waving tops of singular fern-like growths," and thereafter it is nearly always couched in terms of horror. "[O]mnipresent gardens" are "almost terrifying in their strangeness"; "fern-like growths" are "abnormally vast," and some of them exhibit a "ghastly ... pallor"; "great spectral things resembling calamites" rise "to fabulous heights," and entire forests consist of "fearsome growths." Peaslee's repugnance at the "small, colourless and unrecognisable" flowers is barely concealed, while his aversion to "more vivid blossoms" which possess "almost offensive contours" is quite unabashed. The region is all-pervadingly lush, thanks to the climate: "The skies were almost always moist and cloudy, and sometimes I would seem to witness tremendous rains." So life, again, is ensured; it is inevitable. And here is the explanation for Peaslee's curious description of the "great jungles of unknown tree-ferns, calamites, lepidodendra, and sigillaria [that] lay outside the city": he describes how "their fantastic frondage" waved *mockingly* in the shifting vapours" (emphasis added). The daemon Life (as personified by Lovecraft in "Ex Oblivione") is thumbing its nose at Peaslee: whether you like it or not, it declares, I will call forth my numberless progeny for their brief and desolate hour!

But even worse than the inevitability of life is its realized presence. "The real horror began," writes Peaslee, "in May, 1915, when I first saw the living things." What Peaslee sees are the members of the Great Race, whose "monstrous outlines" he traces "with uncomfortable ease." Also discernible is an abundance of fauna, which significantly is of a conventionally repellent sort: "The ground and swamps were constantly alive with snakes, lizards, and crocodiles, while insects buzzed incessantly among the lush vegetation." Peaslee's trip through the oceanic depths reveals "living horrors of awesome magnitude" and generally a "wealth of crinoid, brachiopod, coral, and ichthyic life which everywhere abounded." In other words, Peaslee discovers life everywhere, and everywhere he finds it horrific. This latter point, depending as it does on Peaslee's interpretation, may fly in the face of professorial detachment, but then, Peaslee is no mere recorder of bland scientific data. Indeed, for him a fact is not just fact—it is a "full, hideous fact." Peaslee, for better or worse, cannot help but to see the significance of these facts, and ultimately it is this significance, this fullness of "terrible meaning," which urges their communication. Thus we have the horror-laden adjectives and adverbs, which in the final analysis are sure expressions of the hideous-life pessimism that informs so much of Lovecraft's work. Peaslee gives us a picture of a planet—nay, a cosmos—literally teeming with life, and yet he never once turns Nietzschean to bless it with a world-transfiguring Yes. Why does he reject this? Why is all this life, this astonishing abundance, cause for terror? Why are "chronicles" of alien intelligence "frightful" and "annals" of other worlds "horrible"? Why does Peaslee say that he "shivered at the mysteries the past may conceal, and trembled at the menaces the future may bring forth"? The answer to all of these questions is that he perceives in life itself a *perniciousness*, which, put differently, is nothing less than life's aimless course in (consecutive) time, the pointless succession of individual by individual, species by species, alien race by alien race, until the utter end, when all of them, including a feeble and featherless humanity, are reduced to nothing. So when Peaslee says, near the conclusion of the narrative, that if his dreams be true (and in the tale they surely are), then "there is no hope," he is certainly correct. There is indeed no hope: existence is vain.

III. Being, Becoming, and Meaning

The vanity of existence, observed Schopenhauer, finds expression in the whole way in which things exist; in the infinite nature of Time and Space, as opposed to the finite nature of the individual in both; in the ever-passing present moment as the only mode of actual existence; in the continual Becoming without ever Being; in constant wishing and never being satisfied; in the long battle which forms the history of life, where every effort is checked by difficulties, and stopped until they are overcome. Time is that in which all things pass away; it is merely the form under which the will to live—thing-in-itself and therefore imperishable—has revealed to it that its efforts are in vain; it is that agent by which at every moment all things in our hands become as nothing, and lose any real value they possess. (*Studies in Pessimism* 19)

Peaslee holds in his hands the tablet of his dreams, his "prize," which, appropriately enough, shortly becomes "as nothing," lost somewhere in the subterranean ruins during his frenzied flight from nameless horrors. But its soul-shattering significance is not lost. "If the thing did happen," Peaslee equivocates at the opening of the novella, "then man must be prepared to accept notions of the cosmos, and of his own place in the seething vortex of time, whose merest mention is paralysing." The book which slips from Peaslee's grasp has confirmed what he suspected, namely, the actuality of his dreams; the existence of the book, and its exhibition of characters in the English language and in his own hand, has raised dream to the level of reality. Donald R. Burleson (136) has termed the theme behind this instance, and others like it in Lovecraft, as oneiric objectivism. Let us, however, put this on its head and assert that the book may just as well be seen as lowering reality to the level of dream. The book makes the 'real' objectively oneiristic, which simply means that existence is far more tenuous than Peaslee and the rest of his kind ever supposed. "We have woken and we shall wake again," wrote Schopenhauer; "Life is a night filled by a long dream that often becomes a nightmare" (*Early Manuscripts* 15).

But the paralyzing effect of the Lovecraftian nightmare has been challenged. K. Setiya, for instance, has raised the issue of how knowledge of cosmic indifference can possibly be as horrible as Lovecraft in his fiction makes it seem: "it's quite hard to believe seriously that someone could be driven insane merely be realising the indifference of the cosmos" (22). Perhaps so, but we should not forget that

Lovecraft's protagonists do not arrive at this knowledge just through leisurely reflection (as would his readers); they palpably experience it. In fact, one could say that they experience it in the same way a dying man would experience the end of everything he ever loved, including life. Such a person would know what it means to die: he would understand (to paraphrase Tolstoy [674]) not just with his mind but with his whole being.

Peaslee understands with his whole being--and that is why he calls this knowledge "paralysing"—but what does he understand? Quite simply this: that the human species is transient—it is, in an instant, lost "in the seething vortex of time." His crisis, then, is not especially unique, for he has simply raised the knowledge of death to the power of the species. Peaslee is the spirit of the species apprehending its own dissolution, and like the individual who beholds a death and is dismayed by the nonsense that this makes of life, Peaslee sees in the transience of the human race the utter nonsense that is made of its entire existence. Peaslee is a Pascal without God or soul: "When I consider the short duration of my life, swallowed up in the eternity before and after, the little space which I fill, and even can see, engulfed in the infinite immensity of spaces of which I am ignorant, and which know me not, I am frightened" (61)—except that here "my life" is nothing less than the "the human race." In the same spirit he could have said with Tolstoy: "I want to know the meaning of my life, but that it is a fragment of the infinite, far from giving it meaning, destroys its every possible meaning" (689). The meaninglessness of existence is its "vanity"; but in the narrative a subtle irony is present in the way it pictures this vanity, and that brings us back to my hypothesis of the world in the transcendental present. The irony is that a kind of meaning for existence is possible. Let me explain.

The world as ultimately conceived in "The Shadow out of Time" is without a temporality of consecutiveness; time is reduced to a mere dimension of space. From the time-traveling capability of the Great Race we can infer that whatever is real, is real Now—that is to say, the present is real Now, the past is real Now, and the future is real Now. But the Great Race alone has extensive (though not total) access to the coexistent reality of the transcendental present. All other conscious life-forms are confined to the reality of an empirical now, a now, that is, whose content rapidly rushes past as the stream of time. But these life-forms also pass away in time, even though in truth there is no passing away: all that is real, is real in the transcendental present. From that standpoint there is no such thing as transience; every real event exhibits itself eternally beside every other real event, and thus the human race, as one such event, would never actually be lost.

The problem is that reality as such, standing firm and unchanging, is not knowable to the human intellect. Peaslee, of course, approaches it during mind-exchange, but even then he instinctively compre-hends the experience in terms of a temporality of consecutiveness: he gives it a date (1908) and duration (five years), acts which pathetically demonstrate the innate and unalterable limitations of human knowl-edge. (One is also reminded of Peaslee's anachronistic attempts to measure the architectural structures of the Great Race in "feet"— call it an all-too-human spatiality). Given this, there is no way that Peaslee could ever hope to grasp in any authentic manner the 'truth' that the human race does not vanish in "the vortex of [consecutive] time" but that it actually abides forever in the "eternity" of the tran-scendental present. This 'truth' is by nature not accessible to him and to human experience generally. Humankind will never experience its own imperishability just as no human individual will ever experi-ence physical immortality. As such the 'truth' of our everlastingness is quite useless—whether as theory or solace—and so indeed would be any truth manifesting itself at this fundamental level of reality, including a truth about meaning.

The inaccessibility of the meaning of existence presumes, obviously, that there is a meaning, and as I've said one is in fact possible. The only theoretically intelligible meaning, however, would be *immanent*. In other words, if one could apprehend the world, reality as a whole, in the light of the transcendental present, in which all time is reduced to space and every event is side by side and all at once, one could know where any given part of existence, no matter how apparently trivial, 'fits' in the context of the whole; and this perspective, which would of course require extraordinary intellectual power, could furnish the kind of background that Lovecraft believed gave meaning to human life.

> Despite all careless talk of individuality and self-sufficiency, it is really only as part of a pattern that man can effectively envisage himself as a significant object. Take away all reference-points and he is lost. It is only against the background which stretches around and behind him that he is able to attain any sense of placedness, meaning, purpose, direction, or interest. (*Miscellaneous Writings* 191)

What Lovecraft is referring to here is tradition (Mariconda 5), but tradition is grounded in familiarity (*Miscellaneous Writings* 190); and from the standpoint of the transcendental present, and with an intellect capable of extending the field of the familiar ad infinitum, a meaningful cosmic background could be producible, though, as I've noted above, it would be absolutely incomprehensible to humanity. Nevertheless this would constitute an immanent meaning of existence.

Perhaps the Great Race has grasped the immanent meaning of existence, or, rather, perhaps they are attempting to grasp it. But even if they succeeded, and even if they could communicate it to Peaslee (for instance), it would not be much consolation for most people. It would answer the inquiry "Why is 'anything'?" (e.g., "Why is the Great Race?", "Why is Peaslee?", "Why is Mackensie's typewriter?", etc.), but it would not answer the question "Why is *everything*?"; and the answer to this question, which would impart the *transcendent* meaning of life, is what most people are after and what most religious and transcendent philosophies presume to supply. Given the way the world is in the narrative, an understanding of the transcendent meaning of existence would require a perspective from outside the cosmos and from beyond the realm of the transcendental present, and this apparently is not attainable even by the Great Race which is confined to existence as given in the light of that present. But in any case the text restricts itself to an immanent meaninglessness. Peaslee's discovery penetrates only this layer of vanity, a fact which, incidentally, is perfectly consistent with Lovecraft's philosophical attitude in general:

We have no reason to ask the trite questions of "whence, whither, and why", for it is is only our finite, subjective, rudimentary intellects which conjure up the notion of cosmic purpose. According to all the evidence we can command, we came from chaos and will return to chaos; drifting in a blind mechanical cycle devoid of anything like a goal or object. (*Miscellaneous Writings* 146)

Perhaps "The Shadow out of Time" never bothers with transcendent meaning (the ultimate function or purpose of the cosmos as a whole) because it so firmly establishes the human incapacity to grasp immanent meaning (the ultimate function or purpose of any particular thing in the cosmos). If the latter is inaccessible, then how can we ever expect to seize the former? All that we know is the placid island upon which we rest, an island surrounded by an ocean of ignorance, of "chaos," and because of this we cannot hope to gain or hope to state in any terms whatsoever the sense of the world, of existence, of life, so that we may be redeemed from the persistent condition of its utter vanity and worthlessness. This is, in short, the vanity of existence in "The Shadow out of Time" and though the world may not be literally as it is represented in the tale (with time reducible to space and all events coexisting in an imperishable eternity) it still expresses that universal senselessness which every thoughtful individual faces in the realization that he or she is, as Schopenhauer said, just "one of innumerable similar beings that throng, press, and toil, restlessly and rapidly arising and passing away in beginningless and endless time."

Works Cited

Burleson, Donald R. "On Lovecraft's Themes: Touching the Glass." In David E. Schultz and S. T. Joshi, ed. *An Epicure in the Terrible: A Centennial Anthology of Essays in Honor of H. P. Lovecraft*. Rutherford, NJ: Fairleigh Dickinson University Press, 1991. 135–47.

Cox, Arthur Jean. "Some Thoughts on Lovecraft." In Darrell Schweitzer, ed. *Discovering H. P. Lovecraft*. Mercer Island, WA: Starmont House, 1987. 58–64.

Faig, Kenneth W., Jr. "The Parents of H. P. Lovecraft." In David E. Schultz and S. T. Joshi, ed. *An Epicure in the Terrible: A Centennial Anthology of Essays in Honor of H. P. Lovecraft*. Rutherford, NJ: Fairleigh Dickinson University Press, 1991. 45–77.

Joshi, S. T. "The Genesis of 'The Shadow out of Time." *Lovecraft Studies* No. 33 (Fall 1995): 24–29.

Kafka, Franz. "The Metamorphosis." In *The Metamorphosis, The Penal Colony, and Other Stories*. Trans. Willa and Edwin Muir. New York: Schocken Books, 1975. 66–132.

Laurel, Stan, and Oliver Hardy, actors. *Below Zero*. Dir. James Parrott. With Tiny Sanford and Frank Holliday. MGM, 1930.

Lévy, Maurice. *Lovecraft: A Study in the Fantastic*. Trans. S. T. Joshi. Detroit: Wayne State University Press, 1988.

Lovecraft, H. P. *Miscellaneous Writings*. Ed. S. T. Joshi. Sauk City, WI: Arkham House, 1995.

Mariconda, Steven J. "Lovecraft's Concept of 'Background.'" *Lovecraft Studies* No. 12 (Spring 1986): 3–12.

Pascal, Blaise. *Pensées*. Trans. W. F. Totter. New York: Dutton, 1958.

Safranski, Rudiger. *Schopenhauer and the Wild Years of Philosophy*. Trans. Ewald Osers. Cambridge, MA: Harvard University Press, 1989.

Schopenhauer, Arthur. *Early Manuscripts (1804–1818)*. Ed. Arthur Hübscher. Trans. E. F. J. Payne. Vol. 1 of *Manuscript Remains in Four Volumes*. New York: Berg, 1988–90.

———. Studies in Pessimism. In *Essays of Schopenhauer*. Trans. T. Bailey Saunders. New York: Willey Book Company, n.d.

———. *The World as Will and Representation*. Trans. E. F. J. Payne. Vol. 2. New York: Dover, 1969. 2 vols.

Setiya, K., and S. T. Joshi. "Lovecraft on Human Knowledge: An Exchange." *Lovecraft Studies* No. 24 (Spring 1991): 22–23, 34.

Tolstoy, Leo. "A Confession." In *The Portable Tolstoy*. Ed. John Bayley. Trans. Alymer and Louise Maude. New York: Penguin, 1978. 666–731.

Wilson, Edmund. "Tales of the Marvellous and the Ridiculous." 1945. In S. T. Joshi, ed. *H. P. Lovecraft: Four Decades of Criticism*. Athens: Ohio University Press, 1980. 46–49.

HORRORA MINI-MODEL PROTOTYPE

Pre-Painted Snap Together PVC Figures
1) small—takes up little shelf space
2) no glue or paint required
3) easy to assemble
4) comes with base and attractive display box

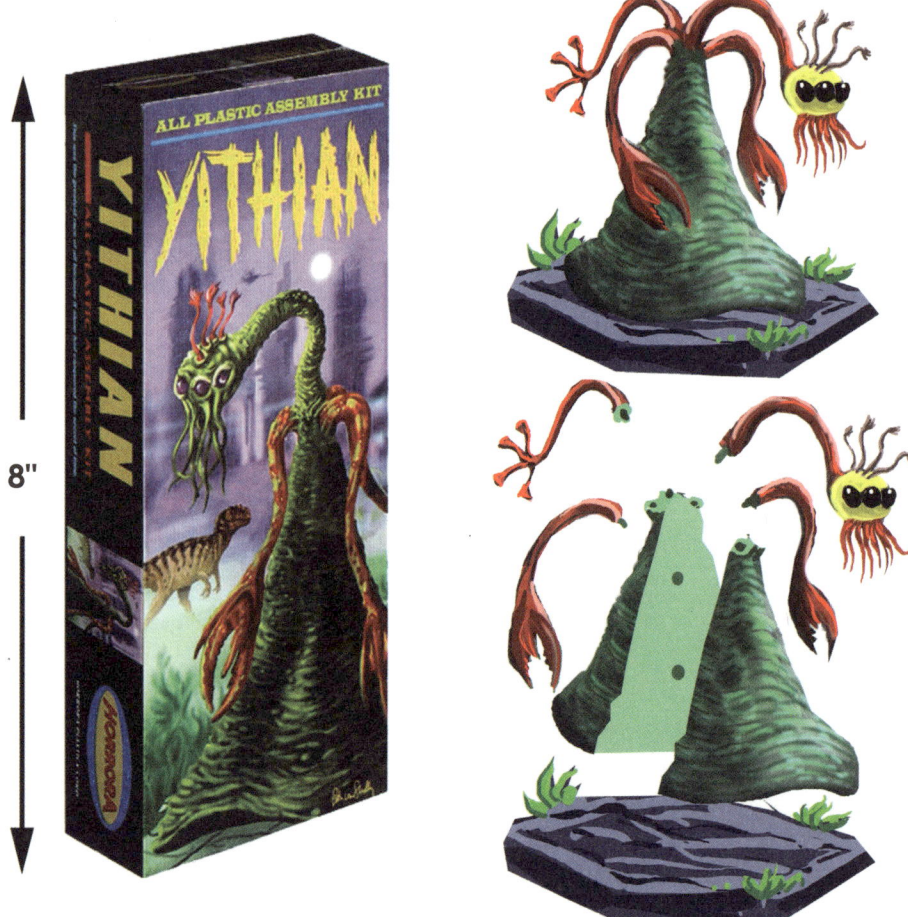

8"

Pitch art for an unproduced snap-together model kit. The Yithian would have been the second kit in Pete Von Sholly's proposed Horrora line through Dark Horse Comics.

The Shadows out of Plastic
by Pete Von Sholly

A few years back I proposed to create a line of model kits through Dark Horse that would represent various monsters and aliens based on their original descriptions in fiction, incorporating all kinds of creations not often seen in their original forms. Unless you read that is!

Most models of this kind were based on monsters as they appeared in movies and television shows. I thought it would be interesting to go back to the sources and produce kits based on what we found in the words of H. P. Lovecraft, Sir Arthur Conan Doyle, H. G. Wells and so forth. Evidently I was wrong! We did produce one such kit in what I hoped would be the "Horrora" line: a shape-changing extraterrestrial as described by John W. Campbell in his classic "Who Goes There?" This is, of course, the tale that spawned the Howard Hawks film *The Thing from Another World* and its remakes. And although the 1982 John Carpenter version did showcase stunning and groundbreaking special effects, and did allow the monster to change shape and become a dog and various people (as opposed to the 1951 version where the monster was just James Arness as a sort of space vegetable Frankenstein monster who changed the shape of his victims but not his own!), they never did get around to showing us Campbell's rubbery, tentacled blue guy with the three blazing red eyeballs! Hence our kit.

I thought it came out great; my wife, Andrea, did a superb sculpt for it, but people like their monster kits from movies they have seen, not from books they have not read, and, sadly, no more kits ensued.

What could have been. A mock-up used to pitch the model kit.

"The Shadow out of Time" as Lovecraftian Horror

by W. H. Pugmire

An idea sometimes expressed is that, had Lovecraft lived and continued writing, he would have completely abandoned writing tales of supernatural horror and concentrated on writing science fiction. I seem to detect (although I may be mistaken) a subtle snobbery in this idea; the thought that writing horror is for dummies, that really smart people write sf. "The Shadow out of Time" is often held up as evidence for this idea of Lovecraft as burgeoning science fictionist; yet it is my contention that the elements of horror are as potent in this story as its ideas concerning cosmic outsidedness. That the story is a masterpiece cannot be gainsaid; that it is also a classic of horror fiction may not be so obvious to some, and yet it contains brilliant elements of what has come to be known as "Lovecraftian horror," a story such as only H. P. Lovecraft could have written. Lovecraft is an American classic of great renown because of his weighty originality, and "The Shadow out of Time" is a product of his unique genius.

The fundamental emotional motif of the story is indeed its element of horror, and of a longing to escape that horror through the manipulation of time. "This idea of a black hidden horror connected with incalculable gulfs of some sort of *distance* was oddly widespread and persistent." That this horror is rooted in *Outside* matters is suggested when, in his attempts to explore and understand its meaning, the narrator becomes intimate "with leaders of occultist groups, and scholars suspected of connexion with nameless bands of abhorrent elder-world hierophants." This is a recurring motif in Lovecraft's weird fiction, a conjoining of cosmic mystery with secrets suggested in antique tomes. We find this in "The Call of Cthulhu," "The Haunter of the Dark," "The Dunwich Horror," &c &c. The mad Abdul Alhazred is indeed a *poet*, yet his songs are more than homage to strangeness in that the pronunciation of his unholy hymns serves to arouse and evoke horrors beyond the rim of mundane time and dimension. The list of these supernatural tomes, now a cliché in Mythos fiction, is found in the text of this cosmic tale – the Comte d'Erlette's *Cultes des Goules*, Ludvig Prinn's *De Vermis Mysteriis*, the *Unausprechlichen Kulten* of von Juntz, the *Book of Eibon* and the *Necronomicon*. One of the chief allures of these sinister volumes is that they are products of the past, and the horrors of which they chant go beyond our puny understand of time, reaching into gulfs of antiquity that defy mortal comprehension.

The manifestation of horror in the story is rooted in this incredible idea of antique time, and that which haunts it. The sheer alieness of the Great Race, similar to that of the Old Ones in *At the Mountains of Madness*, although at first arousing an emotion of terror, transforms into a sense of wonder where the narrators feel a kinship with, and almost an admiration for, these aliens and their societies. The threat to both races comes from other inhabitants of repulsive and petrifying monstrousness, by which the admired alien race will find its eventual extinction. It is this aspect of ultimate horror that serves as motivation in the movement of plot in these tales, and it is the manifestation of that vital horror that gives us two scenes, one in each of the stories, that are among the most terrifying moments in all literature. In *At the Mountains of Madness* we get a wee glimpse of this staggering horror; but in "The Shadow out of Time" we see nothing, yet the experience is no less awesome.

The aspect of horror in this story shews signs of intellectual snob-bery on Lovecraft's part that may be a subtle symptom of his ignorant racism. The alien races in Lovecraft's cosmic fiction are always admi-rably intelligent. The idea of "mind" recurs throughout works such as "The Whisperer in Darkness," "The Shadow out of Time," and (perversely) "Beyond the Wall of Sleep." It is true that the Elder Things in this story are a notch superior to the shoggoths of *AtMoM* and that they are not completely brainless; indeed, "Their minds were of such texture that no exchange with them could be effected by the Great Race." Still, they are presented more as monsters of hideous appetite with their foremost desire being a craving for savage destruction. They are horrors that exist to prey on other beings. Edmond Wilson dismissed them as "invisible whistling octopi" in his notorious condemnation of Lovecraft's fiction, but I personally find the idea of such unseen horrors as powerfully effective. Indeed, Lovecraft had a genius for conjuring pictures of tremendous horror with just a few descriptive lines. One of the most beguiling moments in "The Call of Cthulhu" is when Lovecraft mentions, almost offhandedly, "There were legends of a hidden lake unglimpsed by mortal sight, in which dwelt a huge, formless white polypous thing with luminous eyes." This has always so intrigued me that I wish Lovecraft had written an entire tale concerning that sequestered lake and its monster of legend! I have sometimes toyed with the idea of writing such a tale myself. Part of what makes these horrors so threatening is that they seem to be ruled by murderous appetite alone, sans intellect of any kind.

S. T. Joshi has written of Lovecraft that "…his life as a fiction writer ends, and ends fittingly, with 'The Shadow out of Time'." (*I Am Providence*, page 901). Such a statement seems to dismiss completely that tale of Lovecraft's that is my personal favorite, the Gothic masterpiece "The Haunter of the Dark." The neglect of such a supernatural story such as "Haunter" seems another way in which some critics want to suggest the importance of science fiction in the latter tales of Lovecraft's career.

Part of Lovecraft's originality is that he combined sf elements with supernatural horror and thus invented Lovecraftian horror, and part of what influenced him to do so was his desire to further the market for his fiction, at a time when *Weird Tales* rejected more and more of his work. That Lovecraft began to write with the sf market in mind is undeniable. In describing an idea for a story he had in mind, Lovecraft writes: "I'm not working on the actual text of any story just now, but am planning a novelette of the Arkham cycle—about what happened when somebody inherited a queer old house on top of Frenchmen's Hill & obeyed an irresistible urge to dig in a certain queer, abandoned graveyard on Hangman's Hill at the other edge of the town. This story will probably not involve the actual supernatural—being more of the 'Colour out of Space' type...greatly-stretched 'scientifiction'" (letter to F. Lee Baldwin, 27 March 1934). I think it's safe to say that, no matter how the new genre of science fiction may have affected Lovecraft's literary efforts, had he lived, *supernatural horror* in some manifestation would always be an underlying motif in his fiction.

This new publication of "The Shadow out of Time" illustrated should remind us of the astounding efforts of S. T. Joshi as the editor of Lovecraft's Corrected Texts. This work, which will reach its culmination in the volumes of *The Variorum Lovecraft* to be published by Hippocampus Press, has enhanced Lovecraft's reputation as a brilliant writer, one who succeeded in story after story of achieving his aesthetic goals. It is tragic that Lovecraft went to his grave thinking himself a failure as a writer; but I for one am intensely grateful to Joshi for his respectful treatment of Lovecraft's texts, and for his faithful portrayal of Lovecraft's life and times in such books as *I Am Providence, A Subtler Magick,* and *H. P. Lovecraft: Nightmare Countries.* Combined with volume after volume of the published correspondence of Lovecraft and his friends (I *quiver* with anticipation for the edition of the combined letters of Lovecraft and Clark Ashton Smith!), for which he is assisted in every way by the remarkable David E. Schultz, it is this work that has resulted in H. P. Lovecraft's publication by Oxford, Penguin Classics and The Library of America. Such devotion reveals not only dedication, but a certain kind of genius as well.

THE LOVECRAFT LIBRARY SERIES

The Lovecraft Library Series is the opening salvo from PS Publishing's PULPS imprint—nine uniform dust-jacketed hardcover volumes featuring the very best in cosmic terror from the late great Howard Phillips Lovecraft. These are strictly limited editions of 500 numbered copies, each one resplendent with the breathtaking colour artwork of Pete Von Sholly. Pete has written and illustrated many comic books and magazines for Dark Horse, Last Gasp, IDW, BOOM!, Kitchen Sink and others, and has storyboarded more than 100 feature films including *The Shawshank Redemption*, *The Mist*, *The Green Mile*, *Darkman*, *Mars Attacks!*, *The Mask* and *James and the Giant Peach*. H. P. Lovecraft has been a favourite author of his for many years, and Pete has long wished to visualize his fabulous imagery in book form. And, of course, this is just the beginning! Now, let us begin—but did you lock the door . . . ?

OTHER VOLUMES IN THE SERIES

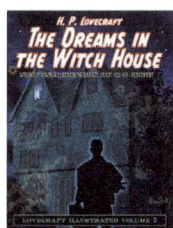

Vol. 1: THE DREAM-QUEST OF UNKNOWN KADATH
(ISBN: 978-1-84863-731-3)

Lovecraft's *Lord of the Rings*—a fantasy epic, full of horror and wonder.

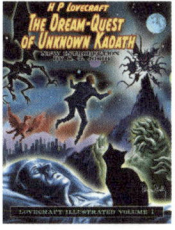

Vol. 2: THE DREAMS IN THE WITCH HOUSE
(ISBN: 978-1-84863-732-0)

A story of sorcery and hyper-space, this is cosmic horror at its finest.

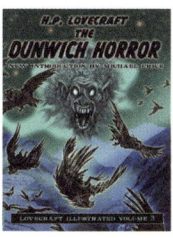

Vol. 3: THE DUNWICH HORROR
(ISBN: 978-1-84863-733-7)

A thing from Outside procreates with an earthly woman to create a monstrous brood destined to destroy our planet. A cornerstone of Lovecraft's fiction.

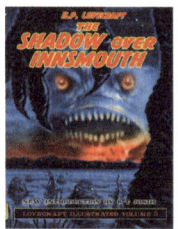

Vol. 5: THE SHADOW OVER INNSMOUTH
(ISBN: 978-1-84863-735-1)

A New England town with hideous secrets lurking in its darkened houses and a dreadful connection with an undersea race whose blood they share.

Vol. 6: AT THE MOUNTAINS OF MADNESS
(ISBN: 978-1-84863-736-8)

Cosmic horror broods and festers in the unexplored frozen wastes while a doomed expedition into a crumbling metropolis stirs the things still lurking in the caverns below.

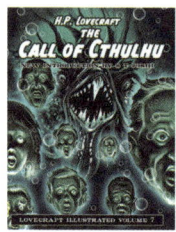

Vol. 7: THE CALL OF CTHULHU
(ISBN: 978-1-84863-737-5)

The story that started it all reveals a titanic ancient being trapped below the sea, biding its time until the stars become right for it and its hordes to rise and reclaim this planet.

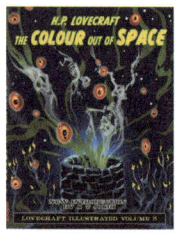

Vol. 8: THE COLOUR OUT OF SPACE
(ISBN: 978-1-84863-738-2)

Something from another part of the universe lands on a new England farm and a hideous life-from begins to spread, warping, dominating and ravaging every living thing it encounters.

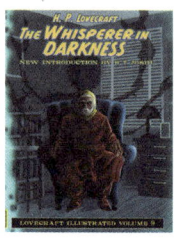

Vol. 9: THE WHISPERER IN DARKNESS
(ISBN: 978-1-84863-739-9)

A tale of the hills and caves of Vermont which are the secret home of a race of beings from the black planet, Yuggoth, and a man who stumbles upon their stunning secrets.